Baby Girl and the Mean Boss

An IR Short Romance

Pepper Pace

Nicole's job at a local diner puts her closer than she likes to her boss Marty--a man more damaged than she is. But one tragic night changes everything

Baby Girl
and the
Mean Boss

Pepper Pace

Baby Girl and the Mean Boss

Baby Girl and the Mean Boss

ISBN-13: 978-1502728807
ISBN-10: 150272880X

Table of Contents

FOREWARD

This story initially appeared on Literotica.com and is also included in a collection of short stories entitled Love Intertwined Vol 1.

ACKNOWLEDGMENT

I find myself acknowledging the same folks in each of my books; the people that have followed my writings at Literotica.com and Blogspot. Without your feedback and encouragement this book would not have happened.

Thanks to my family and friends for their encouragement and patience. I'm sure there were times when I was supposed to be doing things with you but I was preoccupied with my writing.

Chapter One

Nicole hopped off her bike while it was virtually still rolling. Quickly she secured it to the bike rack and hurried into the restaurant, hoping to go unnoticed.

She hated being late for work. Her Boss, Marty, was an asshole. She didn't like giving him a reason to turn his critical eye on her.

She entered through the back door and hurried to the coat rack where she hung up her things. She slipped on an apron and hit the floor.

Marty was at the huge grill, which was his permanent station. Rarely did he allow anyone to take over his realm, which meant he worked almost every day from opening to closing.

Nicole didn't understand him one bit. He owned The Down Home Calabash, but never had the free time to enjoy the benefits of being a business owner. Maybe that's why he was such an ass!

She washed her hands. Marty called over his shoulder without even looking at her.

"You got three orders in Nicole. Stat!"

Annoyed, she thought to herself, 'What do you want, clean hands or quick food?'

Fred was at their shared workstation finishing up a Caesar salad. He worked days while she did nights. Nicole and Fred worked the cold bar and prep station, which other then the grill was *the* most important position in the kitchen. He gave her a big crooked smile, which she returned. The tall lean black man was her best friend at the restaurant—and probably her only friend. He was someone who treated her with the respect that she was unaccustomed to. If she cared to look back on her short but rocky life Nicole would see that all there had ever been was fighting and scratching to survive. Maybe somehow Fred was able to see that because he never missed an opportunity to make life at The Calabash easier for her.

She quickly assessed all the things she was running low on. "Dinner plates!" She yelled over her shoulders. Fred was careful to never let supplies run low for her, but she knew that soon they'd get hit with the dinner rush and she wanted to be sure that she wouldn't run out.

"Thank you!" One of the dishwashers replied. Marty insisted they all use the polite acknowledgement—although he seldom did.

Even though his shift was technically over, Fred continued to help her with the few orders she had waiting. She could have whipped them out easily but appreciated his company. When all of the orders were up, Fred dabbed at his brow with his apron. "Take it easy, Baby Girl, I'm outtie." Fred was only about three or four years older than her. She didn't understand how it was that everyone started calling her Baby Girl, especially when she wasn't even, by far, the youngest female that worked there.

When she asked him once, he smiled and replied that she looked like she should be someone's baby girl.

Somehow that had touched her. He was very wrong. She had never been anyone's baby girl, not even her Mama and Daddy's. She worried after that his treatment and his words meant that he wanted the role, but then she relaxed when she overheard a phone conversation he was having with his roommate and he said he loved him. When he discovered her in the room, his normally handsome face was filled with worry. Evidently it was a secret he wanted kept. Though she felt it wasn't her place to bring it up or to make assumptions, she did have a little pow wow with him behind the restaurant before he left and she promised that it wouldn't be mentioned. Whatever Fred's story was, Nicole never asked...he, like she had never offered up his story. There were certain things friends already knew and didn't need to discuss.

Nicole gave him a quick hug goodbye.

"Two trout dinners!" Marty bellowed.

"Thank you ... " Kendall grumbled. Nicole glanced at her with an amused smile. She knew Kendall was not going to be happy. The young spoiled girl did the food prep for meat, which meant she mostly worked out of the walk-in freezer handling cold, raw meat. It was a job that she thoroughly hated thinking it was too dirty for someone that looked as good as she did. But she was a horrible waitress and wouldn't dream of doing the clean up. The position she had her eye on was Nicole's. Nicole had even offered to swap positions but Marty said no.

Nicole grabbed two dinner platters and prepared them for the trout. She placed them on Marty's wait table and moved on to her next order.

It went like that for the next hour and a half, order upon order with no time to take a breather in between. But Nicole never complained because at least it made the day go faster.

"Nicole, Kendall, take a break." Marty eventually ordered.

It felt just like someone had turned a switch off and she went from ON to instantly exhausted. At least the rush was over for the night. Days like this when she had both college and a full day of work was especially hard.

She and Kendall went out front and found a table out of the way of the waitresses.

"Did you see how many trout dinner's Marty called back?! I mean I got a date tonight and I don't want to be anywhere near some damned raw fish!" Kendall complained. She was twenty-five with long auburn hair and almond shaped green eyes. Nicole thought of Kendall as one of those white girls that thought she was a black girl. She talked like one, dressed like one and even though she was already gorgeous, she probably wished she looked like one.

Nicole shrugged unable to sympathize. In her thirty-two years of life she'd done a lot worse than cut fish. "You are in the wrong job, Kendall," is all she could say. The two weren't quite friends but working closely together for the last two years had allowed them to form a fondness for each other.

11

Kendall made a face. "I'd hate Marty for making me cut fish if he wasn't so damn good looking. Isn't he so sexy?" Oh here we go again, she thought. Kendall had the biggest crush on Marty. Why did so many women gravitate towards the assholes?

Nicole wrinkled her nose and then shrugged. "Marty's not my type."

"How can you tell me that you don't thing he's hotter'n shit?! Don't tell me that you're against in interracial dating." Kendall said pointedly. Nicole was used to her bluntness—it seemed to go hand in hand with her beauty; as if beauty gave her license to be nosey and rude.

It wasn't even worth explaining that her 'type' had nothing to do with looks but with content. "His color has nothing to do with it. It's just him—all him."

Kendall bounced up in her seat, having dismissed their previous conversation. "Oh my god! I can't believe I almost forgot to tell you." Kendall whispered excitedly. "Marty cussed out your boy this morning."

Nicole frowned. "Who?" Her boy?

"Fred."

Her mouth opened in surprise. "Fred? But why?"

"Well, you know how Marty goes into his office and he lets Fred take over?"

"Yeah yeah." Marty might think of himself as superman, but even he had to take a break.

"While he was in his office, one of the regulars complained that her pork chops were tough as leather. It was that old ex-nun lady."

Nicole nodded. The ex-nun was eighty years old if she was a day - and tough as old shoe leather herself. She never tipped more than 50 cents and had even left a nickel once. Nobody liked her...except maybe Marty who would come from behind his fryers to chit chat with her every once in a while.

"Well apparently she had complained about her meal months before and Marty had given her a credit. She tried it again but Fred wasn't biting and he told her that he'd bring her out a fresh order of chops. Of course the old hag had already scarfed them down, so naturally she didn't want anymore. I won't lie, it did get heated, especially when the old hag referred to Fred as boy." Nicole gasped. Marty cursed him out on top of that?

"Anyway, Marty comes out slamming that big ass spatula of his on the pass through. He doesn't even wait until they're in the office before chewing him out. I heard Marty say 'That's bullshit! If she says it was tough then the shit was tough. Who the fuck are you to blah blah blah.'"

Nicole just shook her head incredulously. "You'd think considering that Fred's the hardest worker here, and the only one he trusts to fill in, that he'd give him the benefit. And the very least he could do was take him into the office so he doesn't lose face. Jeez!" She didn't like hearing about her friend being disrespected. It brought back the memory of Nicole's one and only run in with Marty, and the reason that she would never like him.

It was the last Friday before Christmas and it seemed everybody was out finishing up the last minute shopping.   CALABASH being a neighborhood restaurant was popular for its low prices and good food, and it seemed like every customer they'd ever had showed up that day.

They ran out of tomatoes right in the middle of the dinner rush: meaning no salads, no burgers dragged-through-the-garden and B L sandwiches with no T. She grabbed thirty dollars out of the slush fund and sent one of the dish washers to the grocery store. Marty had not had a problem with any of it until he went into the walk-in and found a full box of tomatoes tucked behind a 50 pound tub of pickles.

He bellowed her name so loud that it stopped everyone in the back. Even the waitresses were trying to see what had gotten him upset now. Alarmed, she stopped in the middle of an order to see what he wanted, rushing into the walk-in with him.

"What the hell is this?"   He toed the box in annoyance.

"Oh … I didn't see-"

"And now," He interrupted. "I have thirty dollars worth of hot house tomatoes.

He handed her the heavy bag and walked out letting the door slam behind him.

That had ruined her day. She wanted to crawl under something and lick her wounds. Instead she worked just that much harder. But did Marty acknowledge her additional effort? No.

So, the question was; did she think he was sexy? WHO THE HELL CARED?!   She didn't like being around him so of course she had never looked at him in that way. Besides, it was a documented fact that white men like Marty went for white girls like … Kendall. And in all honesty what man, period, would look at her twice with her quickie ponytail and jeans and t-shirts. Nicole was on a mission and that didn't include trying to be cute.

Grudgingly, though, she had to admit that Marty was a good looking specimen of a man; black or white: tall, muscular physique, shaved head, goatee, tattoo around his bicep, pierced ear and a deep, low sexy voice. His gray eyes were brooding just enough to make anyone-other than her- look twice.

Why was she even thinking about it? Marty was *Marty*!

They finished break and went back on the floor. The rest of the night was pretty quiet but Marty didn't like to see people just standing around. His motto was, 'if you have time to lean, you have time to clean.' Nicole concentrated on cleaning the mini fridge below her workstation. She had to practically get on her hands and knees just to get at everything shoved in the back. She cursed when she came upon a tub of feta cheese, never opened and already past its expiration date.

She chucked the tub into one of the large garbage cans, still on her hands and knees and noticed that Marty was staring at her. She just knew he was going to say something about the unused cheese. But he wordlessly turned back to the grill.

She swabbed out the inside until it sparkled and then neatly restacked everything.

"You know you're the only one that does that." Marty spoke. Nicole glanced up at him.

"Oh, I've noticed." Her reply was mildly sarcastic, because she was still bristling at the idea of him cursing Fred ... and because she *was* the only one that ever cleaned it.

He turned back to the grill without another word.

She was dying to say, 'And you're welcome.'

One thing Nicole liked about the job is that while everybody else had to wait until everything was cleaned before they could go, she cleaned as she went so she could just walk out the door at 11:00.

"See you guys tomorrow." She yelled as she hurried outside.

Nicole hopped on her bike and pedaled furiously down the street. It was her goal to be stepping though her apartment door by 11:15 each night.

Chapter Two

After a long day of classes and working in the hot restaurant, Nicole relished the feel of the wind against her face and the exertion of her thigh muscles as she pedaled to the top of the first hill. Luckily she didn't live far from the restaurant. But she did have to travel on the outskirts of some woods that left her apprehensive, so she always went as fast as she could at night. The pay off was that there were two hills and once she reached the top of the first one the momentum practically carried her to the top of the next one.

As always she had an urge to close her eyes and pretend that she was a bird soaring through the sky. Briefly she gave into the feeling and closed her eyes allowing the exhilaration to surge through her. After the momentum carried her as far as it could Nicole took a deep breath and began pedaling again.

And that's when she saw the SUV make the sharp turn from the darkness of the woods and directly into her path. Almost as if she were detached from herself, she noted the look of shock on the driver's face as the older women realized that she was about to hit her. Briefly, Nicole felt sorry for the driver. She looked like she was someone's mother ... probably one that actually cared...

Nicole's eyes opened slowly. Then she felt a pounding in her head that was magnificent. She blinked, not able to see a thing. Everything was black! Terror instantly engulfed her. She scrambled to sit up but was stopped short by a sudden and sharp pain in her shoulder.

She cried out hoarsely and touched the shoulder carefully. Then in relief she realized that she actually could see. She was outside and it was dark, that's all and the knock on the head had just made everything out of focus. Slowly, she moved her legs. She was sore all over but her legs moved okay. She tried to look around but when her head moved it felt like someone was trying to impale her with a railroad spike. Nicole planted her hand on the ground and pushed herself up into a sitting position clenching her teeth against the pain. Why was she on the ground? Where was she?

With a slow hiss, she let out her held breath then tentatively touched her head. Her hand came away bloody. Nicole felt a wave of nausea at the sight of her bloody hand. It took everything she had not to black out.

As if in a dream, she found herself staring into space and before she realized it time had passed her by. She didn't know how much, or even how she knew that time had passed – only, that she now remembered everything. An SUV had hit her. She couldn't actually recall being hit, just waking up on the ground, bleeding.

Painfully she pulled herself to her feet in a state of shock. She saw her bike a few feet away. One wheel was totally bent. Carefully, she looked around, the initial pain ebbing to a dull throb. Where was the SUV and the nice motherly lady? Had she just left her for dead?

Nicole cried out as her arm moved. She held it to her body to keep it from moving and slowly began walking. The first step was like cut glass in every one of her joints, though after that first step she couldn't much remember pain…she didn't remember anything.

Nicole knew that she must have lost consciousness at some point during the long walk because the next thing she knew is that she was standing at the door of the restaurant. For a moment she felt confusion that she was back here and not home.

From her spot outside of the restaurant, Nicole could see that the interior of THE CALABASH was dark. Everyone had already gone! That meant that it was after one am because after closing it took nearly two hours to clean and to do night prep. Dear god … she'd been hurt for over 2 hours.

Nicole stumbled on her feet as a sob of despair fell from her lips. She was so tired…her eyes welled with tears. She just couldn't walk anymore. Why she had come here instead of home was a mystery, but now that she was here she was too tired to go anywhere else. Nicole leaned against the door, her knees buckling beneath her.

"Ahh!" She cried out. Black spots dotted her vision as she began sliding down the door.

Marty was in no hurry to get back to his empty condo. In fact, he had often times considered bringing in a cot for his office. Hell, his office was more like home to him then his actual home. IKEA had a nice couch that could double as a bed and no one would be all in his business about why there was a cot...

He jumped when he heard a thumping sound at the back door. "What the hell ... ?" Marty stormed through the kitchen, hesitating momentarily as he contemplated grabbing his handgun. But he heard a small mewling sound and his blood almost ran cold.

He barely hesitated as he unlocked the door. Thankfully he had never been robbed. CALABASH was located in a decent residential district. He could hear soft sobs and he carefully pulled open the door. Nicole's crumpled form feel forward. Surprised, Marty reached for her.

"Nicole!"

She screamed in pain when he gripped her shoulder. His face went white at the sound of her scream as well as the sight of her battered form. Without thinking he knelt down beside her, his arm going around her torso where he held her carefully against him.

"What happened?!" His voice sounded and felt like it had turned into dust in his mouth.

Without waiting for an answer he swept her up in his arms, ignoring her cries of pain. Wordlessly, he hurried outside to his truck. Marty placed her into the passenger seat as if she was little more than a baby.

20

Carefully he reached over and pulled a seatbelt across her body. Again she cried out. He blanched even more.

"Take it easy, Baby Girl. Take it easy. I'm going to go lock the restaurant." With trembling hands Marty quickly locked the restaurants doors, dropping the keys once in his excitement. His hands squeezed into fists. Marty cursed himself. How many times had he wanted to offer to drive her home at night? There wasn't a night that went by that he didn't worry that there would be some thug lying in wait for her in those damned woods that she rode past to get to her apartment. And now it had finally happened. When he found out who had done this to her he was going to kill the bastard!

Hurrying back to his truck, he pulled out of the parking lot like a bat out of hell. Slowly Nicole's eyes began to close.

"Nicole! Wake up! Don't go to sleep! Who did this to you?" Marty's gray eyes looked almost dark with anger.

From a distance she heard the question and struggled to clear her head. It was pounding so hard.

"Lady … " Suddenly she was alert. She blinked and cried out in distress. "Marty, she hit me."

"Shhh, shhh. It's okay." He said as he drove, one hand on the wheel, the other gently holding her hand. A lady?? Why would a lady—"Were you hit by a car? Oh god, I thought you'd been … I'm taking you to the hospital."

"My bike … Marty go back and get my bike."

"Nicole-"

"My bike, Marty. Please get my bike," she pleaded.

"Okay." He relented, knowing that he should be rushing her to the hospital, but the pain in her eyes was too much for him to bear. "Where is it?"

"The other way." He did a U-turn in the middle of the road and headed in the opposite direction.

"Nicole ... " He spoke her name more to himself, anxious to get on the track back to the hospital.

It wasn't too long before he saw definite signs of a wreck. He pulled over to the curb and jumped out of the truck. Nicole's bike lay in the middle of the street.

"Jesus ... " He picked up the bike and took a moment to examine it before tossing it into the truck bed. The thing was mangled! He looked around cursing. She had just been left like trash. Marty got back into the truck. Nicole's eyes were closed again.

Baby Girl?" He peered into her face.

"Hmmm ... " She groaned.

"Don't go to sleep." Carefully he touched the back of her head. His hand came away bloody and he could see the blood down the back of her neck and smearing the back of the seat.

He cursed himself for not taking her directly to the hospital. "Hang in there, Baby. Hang in there." Quickly he pulled back into the street and to the hospital.

Nicole felt her eyes closing beyond her control. She just wanted to sleep for a little while ...

"Nicole!" Then they jerked open. "Talk to me, Baby. Tell me about ... the lady." That fucking bitch-ass lady.

"The lady?" She mumbled and looked at him. "What lady?"

"The lady that hit you." Nicole could see the surprised look on the woman's face all over again. Why did she just leave her for dead? Nicole wouldn't leave a dog for dead.

Marty kept looking at her curiously. "Are you with me, honey?"

"My head — stomach … feels weird; heavy."

"When we get to the hospital I'll call your parents-"

Nicole paused. "No." She mumbled. He had to strain now in order to hear her. "I don't have any parents. My Mom passed … I only talk to my Dad at birthdays and Christmas," if then.

He glanced at her again. "What about other family? Friends?"

She hesitated. "Scattered all over the country … Marty … "

"What?"

"I feel funny-" she caught her breath as she felt a sharp pain. Marty pressed the gas, pushing the car dangerously fast.

"Almost there. Funny how?" There was no answer. Thank God the hospital was just up ahead.

Her eyes were closed again. Marty grasped her hand. "It's okay, baby." He pulled into the emergency entrance like he was at the Daytona 500. "We're here. Hang on." Jumping out of the truck, he waved for an attendant.

Chapter Three

The next time Nicole opened her eyes it was daylight. Alarmed, she tried to sit up.

"Hey, hey. Relax." Marty placed a gentle hand on her shoulder. "Don't. You just had surgery."

When she tried to look around her head felt like it had been hit with a sledgehammer and she sucked in her breath.

"You're in the hospital." Marty said quietly. She focused on him. His eyes were red and glassy, his cheeks stubbly with a new growth of beard. "Do you remember what happened?"

She licked her lips. They were dry and hot. "Water ... " She croaked.

"No, Sweetie. You can't have anything to drink. There was internal bleeding. You can have a sponge in your mouth or ice." He reached for a small cup and pulled out a funny little blue object. Carefully he put it in her mouth and it tasted like heaven. She sucked on it, until most of the dryness went away. He took the sponge out of her mouth and placed it back in the cup.

"More."

"No, just one." He picked up a vial. "This might help." He dabbed a finger into the salve and very carefully touched the finger to her lips.

Half asleep, the tip of Nicole's tongue came out to explore his finger. Marty's eyes stared into hers then he quickly looked away.

"It's lip balm." He said clearing his throat. Finally he looked at her again. "How do you feel?"

"Can I go back to sleep?" She said oblivious to her actions.

He smiled. "Yes."

Later Nicole opened her eyes and briefly remembered a different hospital and a different time—happier, a newborn baby in her arms. Painfully she pushed the memory away.

Where was Marty? He had been here, hadn't he? She vaguely remembered him taking away the awful thirst. He had put something in her mouth...a sponge. Nicole licked her dry lips and looked around for the cup with the sponge. There it was on the side table. When she reached for it she discovered that her right arm was in a splint and sling.

With her good hand she touched the back of her head. It was covered in a thick bandage, which made her head feel twice its normal weight. Tentatively she touched her face. One eye was swollen almost closed. Her lips were swollen and she had scrapes on her forehead. Damn, on her forehead? She pressed her hand to her stomach and felt soreness. She pulled down the bed sheet and blanket and lifted the gown slightly. She was naked under the gown and there was an incision covered by clear tape on her side. She studied it in awe before swallowing dryly and remembering that she was thirsty. Noting that in addition to the sling on her right arm she had an IV in the back of her left hand. She greedily stared at the cup wondering how she was going to manage it. Carefully she sat up and when she didn't black out she swung her legs over the edge of the bed so that she could reach the cup.

"Nicole!" Marty was standing in the door holding a Styrofoam cup and a brown paper bag. He hurried to the bed and put his things on the bedside table. "What are you doing? You have a concussion!" He frowned at her sternly. "Come on, lay back down." He took hold of the covers and lifted it just as she swung a leg back onto the bed.

Nicole was exposed from where she'd hiked her gown up to examine her belly and Marty got a perfect view of Nicole's nudity. Quickly he averted his eyes, lowering the covers as soon as she had her legs back onto the bed.

Nicole cringed inwardly feeling her face flame in embarrassment. Not only had she not trimmed her crotch in ages, she also hadn't shown it to a man in years—and then HE, of all people, gets an eyeful. She quickly reached beneath the covers and adjusted her gown as she finished settling in the bed. She avoided meeting Marty's eyes.

When she finally did look at him, she noted that his face was red, also. He cleared his throat and tried to feign nonchalance as he pulled a chair closer to the bed.

"I had to leave for a minute to get coffee." He reached for a cup filled with melting ice. "Ice?"

"Oh yes, Please. I'm so thirsty."

"The medicine will make you feel that way. You sure have had an awful lot of it, too." It seemed as if she had been given everything including the kitchen sink. He grasped a piece of ice and carefully slipped it into her mouth.

"Uhm. That's good." She sighed and savored it, licking her dry swollen lips. He watched mesmerized, eyes focused on her full lips and the way her tongue ran over them, knowing that she was completely unaware of how delicious she made those lips look. Marty silently watched her as he fed her another piece of ice after the first one melted.

For an instant Nicole forgot that this was the same Marty that she and Kendall had been mercilessly calling names. She'd never seen him this nice to anyone. He seemed like a different person. It made her lower her guard, something she would have never done with Marty in the past. Swallowing past her earlier embarrassment, she swallowed the ice morsel.

"How long have I been here? What did they do to me?"

Marty didn't answer immediately. He replaced the cup of ice and picked up his half forgotten coffee. "Two days. Today is Thursday."

Nicole gasped. "I don't remember … "

"Why should you? You've been unconscious. You have a really bad head injury Nicole. Had you been wearing a helmet perhaps you'd be out of here by now." He gave her a stern look and the Marty that she was familiar with was back. "You can *never* do that again. If you ever crack your head in the same spot … "

Her eyes widened. And then suddenly he blinked, and his eyes transformed from a dark storm to his more normal cold gray. "You're going to be okay, Baby Girl." He said with a sigh. "The police need to know about the women who hit you. I tried to give them some information...but I didn't know very much."

"I don't know much myself. I just remember that she looked like a nice, sweet, Motherly type."

"Anybody who'd hit a person on a bike then leave...*isn't* nice." He said with forced control.

Nicole noted how his face instantly darkened and how easily he angered. She forced herself to remember the details so that she could give him the information he wanted.

"She was driving a red SUV. That's all I know. She was a black lady, about fifty-five or sixty."

Marty waited and when she didn't continue he nodded. "Well the police took some paint from your bike-"

"Marty?" Something suddenly dawned on her. "Who's watching the restaurant?"

He didn't answer right away. "I closed it."

"You closed it? You didn't even close it for Christmas." She knew first hand because she had worked it with him. Did that mean that he'd been here for the full two days? Somehow that idea made her feel funny.

A nurse walked in then and was pleased to see Nicole awake. She wanted to take her vitals and when Marty moved to leave, the nurse assured him that she wouldn't be long. She asked Nicole if she thought she could make it to the bathroom and she responded that she could. Marty stood back and watched the nurse help Nicole to the small lavatory, averting his eyes when her gown slipped open and exposed a bit of one milk chocolate butt cheek. Nicole quickly looked over her shoulder to see if Marty had caught sight of that but he had been quicker and was already pretending to watch the television screen that sat suspended on the adjacent wall.

Ten minutes later she was in bed, settled and tucked in. Her head pounded like tom toms from the effort, though.

"Are you in any pain?" The nurse asked.

"Yes." She said between clenched teeth.

"I'm going to put some medicine in your I.V. You'll be sleeping like a baby in no time."

Nicole watched the nurse inject the narcotic tensely. What was the protocol? Did she say no, I'm a recovering addict? Please don't give me that drug and make me remember how I used to crave that high...

The nurse, misunderstanding her agitation, gave her hand a brief pat. "You'll be better very soon. I'll send the doctor to look in on you later." Then she left.

"Nicole," Marty leaned forward. "The other day when I asked you about family, you said that you had none. What about friends? Is there anybody that could take care of you when you get out of the hospital?"

"Take care of me?" Her response was surprised. The concept was foreign since she'd been taking care of herself her entire life.

"I don't mean take care of you...I just mean somebody to keep an eye on you. You almost died ... I'm not trying to scare you, Nicole, but I do want you to understand how serious this is." Marty's eyes looked distant. "You lost so much blood-"

Nicole carefully drew in her swollen lip. "Marty, I can take care of myself." There was not another word spoken for almost a full minute.

Marty sighed. "I'll be back later." He got up and left without a backward glance.

Nicole felt a sudden emptiness. She knew that Marty was taking her response, or lack thereof, as stubbornness. It wasn't. There just wasn't anybody that Nicole could count on. She couldn't go home to family that didn't exist. Nicole felt fear. Not of what was happening to her, but of the familiar solitude. He did not understand that even if there was a family they wouldn't want her. They wouldn't take care of her. They never had in the past and they wouldn't now.

Chapter Four

Hours later she heard the door open. The drugs had put her into a fuzzy little cocoon. It had been years since she had acquainted herself with narcotics... and what scared her was that she was enjoying it.

Nicole surprised herself further when she was disappointment that it was a Doctor entering her room and not Marty. It gave her a moment of pause to think that she was actually missing Marty's company. In a million years she would have never dreamed that would be possible.

The Doctor examined her, poking and prodding. They talked at length about her injuries and it seemed to Nicole that he was being intentionally vague. Every question she asked was met with the same response: 'We won't know until you heal'. In other words, I have no idea, just guessing here.

Her worst injury was the head injury that could have long terms affects on her health...of course when she asked what kind of long term effects, the Doctor rambled off a lot of technical terms until her head began to swim.

"I think you should be able to eat solids and drink liquids." Her cracked and dried lips did appreciate that! Nicole suddenly put her concerns behind her at the thought of a cool cup of water.

She was eating soup when the door opened again. Marty walked in and Nicole felt herself smile cheerily before she quickly hid it. He was all cleaned up and wearing fresh clothes. For the second time in a week Nicole took a moment to admire his good looks, remembering the first time she'd seen him. She had stopped in the restaurant for a cup of coffee. Having just that day, moved into her small efficiency apartment, she was happy to see a restaurant within biking distance. Taking a seat at the bar she felt her stomach grumble as she sipped the coffee, enjoying the aroma that wafted from the kitchen and wishing that she had more than five dollars to spend.

Amid all of the pleasant chatter, stood one silent man that seemed absorbed in flipping one thing, deep frying something else, placing orders up on the pass thru. She watched as he yanked down one order, filling it with quiet efficiency. Big was her first thought; he was tall and thickly built with solid muscles, though not like a body builder, more like a sleek linebacker.

After finishing her coffee and breaking down to order a slice of lemon meringue pie that tasted like heaven and was obviously homemade, Nicole had asked the waitress if they needed any help. She had never worked in a restaurant before, but she knew what hard work was...and working backline with Marty was about as hard as it got.

After her breath jaunt down memory lane, Nicole curiously watched him enter the room. He had a shopping bag in his hands.

"How do you feel?"

She reached for the remote control of the television set and turned down the volume.

"Better. Sore. The doctor took out my I. V. And, I can eat and drink now."

"Good. I talked to him a minute ago. He said that I should be able to get you out of here tomorrow."

"That soon?" She asked, nervously.

"You'll be okay." He assured her. "I went home and showered and brought you some of my sweats and a t-shirt to wear home." He gestured to the shopping bag.

Nicole's brow went up in surprise. "Thanks, Marty. I wish I could get cleaned up, too ... I still have blood all over me."

"Maybe you can." He buzzed the nurse. When she responded he asked about a shower. She didn't see any reason why not.

Marty watched as the nurse removed the splint and brace. She carefully unwrapped the bandage from Nicole's head. It was matted and tangled with dried blood. It disgusted her and she wished Marty wasn't there to see it. He took his cue and eased out of the room making some vague statement about making a phone call.

The nurse wouldn't leave Nicole alone in the shower so she made it a quickie. It still felt good, but it scared her to see all the blood pooling around her feet.

Painfully she got into a fresh gown and the nurse helped her to replace the brace.

"I'll be back in a jiff with fresh bandages and I'll have your boyfriend come back in."

"Oh ... that's not ... " Nicole felt her cheeks flush. "Thanks." She mumbled.

When Marty came back in he stared at her hair. It was washed and cleaned but a mess all over her head. What could she do about it, though? She had just discovered that she had forty stitches crisscrossing the back of her head!

The nurse had left her with a very inadequate hairbrush. Using her good left hand she carefully dragged it through the tangle of curls.

Marty grimaced along with her. "Careful ... "

"I'm trying-" She replied, feeling her face grow hot.

"Here give it to me." She looked at him uncertain but he took the brush out of her hand and tentatively began to brush the ends, gently gripping the length in his fist to avoid tugging the stitches. "Okay?"

She nodded and he continued.

Nicole was wide-eyed with shock. Kendall should be seeing this. This is truly unreal...Marty is doing her hair. Maybe she was still unconscious and this was all a freaky dream ...

"Marty?"

"Yeah?" He mumbled in deep concentration at his task.

"This is very weird ... "

He chuckled. "Please don't tell anybody at work." She liked the sound of that chuckle. It wasn't something he did often.

"Why are you being so nice to me?" She asked seriously.

He paused in his struggle with her hair. "Why wouldn't I be?"

She turned carefully and looked up at him. "I appreciate it, I really do. I just don't understand...why you've stayed with me." It embarrassed her to ask it in such a blunt way, but she truly didn't understand. Marty was as cold and distant as they came; mumbling his greetings and finding fault easily. He was sarcastic and could curse a blue streak at the drop of a dime. On top of that he had a temper and was known to throw food, dishes, and spatulas when he was pissed. So, to see him brushing her hair with painstaking gentleness was – to say the least – disturbing.

His gray eyes stared into her brown ones. Something stirred in Nicole; warmth, something she hadn't felt in a long time.

"I feel partly responsible for what happened to you."

That surprised her. "But why?"

"Because you're on a bike—at night—alone."

"Why would you be responsible for that?"

"Because … " He looked uncomfortable. Gently he turned her head back around so that he could continue brushing her hair. "Because you work for me and when you leave my establishment it should be safe for you to get home. I don't think riding your bike in all weather, at night is particularly safe."

"You've...thought about this before?"

"Yeah. I think about all you guys...even if you all think I'm just plain mean."

Nicole turned back around. His face was its normal stern but she saw a twinkle in his eye. Did he always have that twinkle? Was that how it really was with

Marty? He wore a cold mask but it was only hiding that twinkle?

Chapter Five

The door opened and the nurse returned with a tray of antiseptic and gauze. With an approving smile she nodded at the sight of Marty grooming Nicole. "You're lucky, Sweetie, to have such a good boyfriend. He never left your side once when you were unconscious." Marty put down the brush but didn't so much as open his mouth to correct the nurse's assumption. Nicole kept her eyes lowered, confused and uncomfortable.

The nurse cleaned and applied salve to her stitches. When she was finally finished torturing her poor scalp, she announced that they wouldn't need bandages and warned her to clean the stitches once a day.

How was she supposed to do that? She had shoulder length hair that was like a 1960s afro right now! She guessed that she should be thankful that she hadn't had to get her head shaved. Not that she really cared about such things. The last thing she cared about was her looks.

After the ordeal, Nicole had a killer headache and the nurse left leaving her more painkillers.

Marty watched her as she grimaced trying to find a comfortable pillow arrangement for her head. Without being asked he plumped her pillow and adjusted her covers. Nicole stared at everything but him with a mixture of confusion and gratitude. For the first time the silence was awkward between them.

She was reluctant to meet Marty's gaze, because he was just standing there looking down at her; all muscled out in his t-shirt and recently shaved head and face. It wasn't far-fetched; the nurse's assumption that Marty was her man. He was acting like a very devoted boyfriend. Much more devoted then James had when she had last been in the hospital giving birth to their child. Marty cleared his throat and she finally looked up coming back to the present.

"Nicole, do you have insurance?"

She didn't know what she had expected but it wasn't that. The question had come out of clear blue and had shocked her so much that she had almost asked him if he offered health insurance because she sure missed that on the application for minimum wage backline cook! She caught herself in time.

"I have a medical card."

"A medical card?" He asked confused.

She gave him a long look. Yeah she had been on welfare, and still continued to receive aid for college. She tossed him a half truthful answer. "I had to apply for it when I got the state assistance for college."

"Like welfare?" She could feel his judgment of her, and it stung.

"Not like ... *is* welfare." She sank into her bed and pulled the covers up to her chin defensively. "Some people can afford college with their trust funds and good jobs." She looked at him pointedly. "Most of us aren't lucky enough to have those things." A half beat passed in which she thought Marty was going to swoop down and bite her head off.   Instead he blinked confused.

Instantly she regretted her words. How could she be so insulting when Marty had been so kind? But instead of chewing her ass he never responded to her harsh words.

"I'll take your medical card down to the billing office so that we can get checked out tomorrow with no hold ups."   That statement made her feel even more like a shit.

"It's in my wallet, in my jacket pocket ... wherever my jacket is." She said contritely.

"Your jacket is pretty much ruined."   She watched him walk to a small closet. Her coat was stuffed into a clear plastic bag. He rummaged around until he came up with her wallet.   Without even a glance in her direction he opened it and began rifling around in it. Nicole kept her mouth clamped shut but she wanted to tell him to stop looking at her personal items and that he was nosey...but she knew deep down that it wasn't so.

Her eyes began to drift close. She wanted to apologize for being so bitchy but couldn't figure out how to do it without making an already tense situation worse. She'd just tell him thanks ...

He glanced up from her wallet to her sleeping form. "Sleep tight, Baby Girl. I'll be back tomorrow."

She thought she might have said goodnight in return ... but maybe not.

The next day was a bright and beautiful Friday. Nicole could not believe that she had spent most of this week in the hospital.

She dressed in the overly large clothes that Marty had left for her. Still not able to manage with the brace the nurse had to assist her. Neither was able to locate her bra and panties and she had a fleeting concern that Marty had taken them. But then she felt ashamed. More likely they had to be cut away.

Marty walked through the door right before noon.

"Sorry I'm so late-" Late? When everything he did was of his own volition.

"Did you open the restaurant?" She asked.

"Yeah. Fred's holding the fort."

Nicole made a humphing noise. "Good thing you didn't fire him."

"What?"

Again she felt a flash of shame. What in the hell was wrong with her?! Marty had been going out of his way to help her. "Nothing," she got out of bed while he stepped out the door and returned with a wheelchair.

She gave him a surprised look. "Oh no-"

"Sorry, Baby Girl. It's the rule." He helped her sit down and noticed that her shoes weren't on. Kneeling in front of her he slipped them on and tied the laces efficiently. Damn, he had a big neck, she thought in admiration. She liked her men on the thicker side ... what?! Stop it, she chastised herself.

"Ready?"

"You wouldn't believe how."

As she waited for him to open the passenger door to his truck, Nicole wondered if she had left any permanent stains on the seat. She'd have the car reupholstered if she had. No matter if it cost her two months salary! She was pleased to see when he helped her inside that the seats were sparkly clean. She didn't mention it.

He pulled her seat belt on, careful about the injured shoulder then he quickly hopped in.

The drive was silent for the most part although Marty periodically glanced in her direction.

She noted that he was taking a strange route to her apartment. He pulled up to the driveway of a condo—a nice one.

"Where's this?" She asked.

"My place." He got out of the truck and opened her door. She looked at him in confusion and then took his offered hand and climbed out of the truck.

"What are we doing here?" Marty took her arm and led her up the walk.

"You'll see."

Oh please, don't let this be some surprise welcome home party. With all the activity of leaving the hospital, her head was starting to ache. Reluctantly she allowed herself to be guided inside.

Marty's home was very nice. And there was no one in sight. She looked at him confused. Silently he led her into a living room decorated comfortably in muted earth tones. He helped her sit down in an oversized armchair and then he sat on the sofa across from her.

"You're staying here."

Chapter Six

The expression on Nicole's face spoke more than words ever could. He continued quickly before she could object.

"Now, I've thought about this Nicole. You can't be by yourself these first couple of days. Someone needs to care for your stitches-"

"Marty, I can't-"

He stood up. "Yes. You can. I've made up the spare room for you-"

She was shaking her head, which wasn't a good idea with the intensifying headache. "I appreciate it Marty. I really do! But-"

He kneeled on his haunches in front of her and touched her hand. Reluctantly he spoke the words that he had hoped he would not have to. "Nicole, you don't realize how close you came to dying. I didn't want the doctor to dwell on that with you because I didn't think it would help you to know." His expression grew apologetic. "I had to pretend to be your...boyfriend in order to get any information out of him." He sighed. "Baby...your head shattered. They want you wearing a helmet for 4 weeks just so that if you fall you won't..."

What?! Nicole's mouth opened and then closed, heart thudding in her chest anxiously. "Wha-? Shattered?"

Marty licked his lips just sick at having to tell her this, and at the look of fear on her face. "I don't want to scare you. But because of your skull fracture," he shook his head then looked at her carefully, "you black-out all the time; several times a day. But you don't seem to know it." Nicole's eyes squeezed closed and then open as streaks of pain shot through her head. Just the confusion of information was impossible to absorb and now her head was freaking killing her. Besides, it wasn't her head that was causing her to black out, if that is what she was doing. It was the drugs. She was just blacking out because she was on the nod, right? She didn't even know how to form words to explain that but couldn't because that was her business not his.

Nicole tried to reach up to rub her throbbing head but couldn't. Her mind was trying to grasp the information that he had just told her. Had the doctor said anything about blacking out? He'd mentioned seizures but said they should go away…only she hadn't had any so didn't think about his words. But had she been having seizure all alone? How in the hell was this going to impact her life? Would she just freaking keel over during her day to day life? She briefly closed her eyes as sharp, pains shot through her skull, forgetting about Marty for the time being. Each beat of her heart seemed to amplify it. She was trying to reach up with her arm in the sling, not remembering why she couldn't do it.

"Are you okay?" Marty asked.

"My head … "

"You need to lie down," he insisted.

"I'll be okay … " She tried to tell him that she didn't want to lie down anywhere except in her own bed, in her own apartment but she couldn't think clearly enough to form the words.

"Nicole?" She was just staring into space like she'd been hypnotized.

Marty paled. "Nicole!" He waved his hand in front of her face. His heartbeat quickened. She was having a seizure.

Marty cursed the woman that had done this to Nicole for the millionth time. If the cops ever found the woman—old motherly type of not—she was going to be sorry!

In opposition to his rage, Marty gently lifted her into his arms and carried her upstairs. He lay her down in the spare bedroom, pulled her shoes off and carefully tucked the covers around her. Her eyes still stared into empty space; vacant but periodically blinking.

He watched her for a while wanting to do so much more to help her...How many times had he secreted looks at Nicole as they worked the back line together. Over the last few days, as she healed, he had been able to watch her to his heart's content, but there was no joy in seeing her broken like this.

How could this be the same woman that had walked into the restaurant with wild curls held back by sunglasses and a beat up jeans jacket. He had scanned her application quickly, appreciating her height and well-proportioned thickness. And he had thought that she looked enough like that actress from the movie Love and Basketball that he had taken a second look.

She was pretty in an understated way. No make-up, no jewelry, not even a purse. She walked through the door with her hands shoved into the pockets of her jeans and looked around warily. It was like her best friend had run off with the last of her money...that look in her eyes stayed with him long after he should have dismissed her.

Chapter Seven

Later, after he had hired her to work the backline, he had teamed her up with Fred knowing that she had already surpassed most of the people that worked for him by not whining, stealing or trying to fuck him. He also wanted her working the backline so that he could monitor that look; identify if it would disappear, if there was another expression that didn't contain so much pain. There was.

Her smile.

Her smile was few and far in between. But even fewer was her laughter. One day Fred had whispered something to her and she had smiled and bells suddenly seemed to fall from her lips and it sounded like angels were laughing. He was not prepared for the stab of jealousy when that laugh was directed at Fred.

Marty shook his head to clear his thoughts and he realized that he was just standing there staring at her. He clenched his teeth. He was simply too angry to witness the effects of the accident on her. He turned to leave, closing the door softly behind him.

Later, when Nicole awakened she had no idea where she was. It wasn't the hospital because she was much too comfortable. She pushed a wonderful chenille blanket off of her and stood on shaky legs looking around her.

The room was fairly large; double bed, side tables, an armchair and a small antique dresser that had flowers and cards on it. Slowly she walked over to the dresser and sniffed the flowers. She picked up each card and read them smiling. They were from her coworkers wishing her a speedy recovery and addressed to *Baby Girl*.

She noticed two shopping bags on the floor and explored them curiously. They contained some of her clothes from home. When Marty had gone through her wallet he had also taken the key to her apartment. She shook her head in disbelief. Marty had gone to her apartment? It was thoughtful and disturbing all at the same time. Feeling somewhat violated, she slipped on her shoes. Where was he, anyway? Regardless of his good intentions, he was going to take her home now!

She went downstairs with a purpose but couldn't help admiring his spacious home. He had a fireplace! This was nothing like her small little efficiency. Her face tightened. She wasn't about creature comforts. She had a mission and that was to get educated and then paid. Once she fulfilled her vow to her daughter maybe then she could look at herself in a mirror again.

Briefly, Nicole closed her eyes. Alicia was a memory she did not allow herself to often enjoy.

Something smelled good and she felt her stomach grumble. She'd had slimy oatmeal at the crack of dawn and dried toast with a pat of congealed butter substitute on it. She went into the kitchen.

Wow! It was impressive! Marty was at the stove concentrating, much like he did when he was at work. He looked surprised when he saw her standing there. He moved a skillet from the burner and turned off the fire.

"How do you feel?"

"Better. My head stopped hurting...mostly." She sighed.

"Sit down." He said helping her to a barstool. "The headache must have been a trigger for the seizure." She looked at him confused.

"What seizure?"

He stared at her with the same confused look absently fingering the small kokopelle that he always wore tied around his neck.

"Uhm ... do you remember what we were talking about...before?"

"Yeah." Her eyes were wide with the obviousness of that question. "About me going home." Marty sat down on the barstool next to her.

"And?"

"She shrugged, "And what?"

"And how did you get from the living room to the bedroom?"

"I ... " Nicole's brow furrowed. How is it that she had never considered how she'd moved from talking to Marty in the living room to sleeping in the spare bedroom? As she tried to remember there was nothing there...just a blank spot in her memory. She looked at Marty, her chest moving up and down in confused panic.

49

"I was telling you-" He stopped short, not wanting to speak those hurtful words again. "You had a seizure and I took you upstairs."

Nicole's eyes were suddenly sharp and frantic. "I had a seizure?" She trembled. Seizure, seizure…that's right! The head injuries caused blackouts. And maybe it wasn't the fact that she had been reintroduced to drugs during her stay at the hospital? Did that mean she was brain damaged? What if she blacked out at school, riding her bike, walking up the stairs…She couldn't remember doing it … what other things was she forgetting? What if she forgot to turn off the stove-?

Marty saw all of these thoughts cross her face. Nicole probably never realized that her thoughts played across her face like loud speakers and Marty always knew her mood; annoyed, tired, wishful…and very seldom happy. He placed a reassuring hand on her shoulder and she looked at him with frightened eyes. He swallowed back a desire to punch a wall.

"Nicole. You will be all right. Give yourself time to heal…and let somebody help take care of you, just for the time being. Baby, what if this had happened while you were alone?"

Her mind latched onto that word *baby*. It was different without the word *Girl* attached to it. He'd called her Baby … and it wasn't the first time was it? Something about her head … and then the entire conversation flooded back.

Marty could see that she remembered as her body shuddered. Her caramel complexion suddenly colored red and tears appeared in her eyes. He pulled Nicole into his arms when those tears spilled down her cheeks. He couldn't stop himself. He just couldn't.

Marty found himself planting kisses on her head. "I'm here. Sssh. It's going to be okay." Then he rocked her gently in his arms. "I'm going to take care of you. I promise."

She was so tired; physically and mentally. For once in a long time she held onto someone else as if it was a lifeline. It had been so long since someone had comforted her. Marty's arms were so big and protective. As gruff as he sometimes sounded, Nicole was beginning to understand that he was equally as harmless. She hid her face against his chest, inhaling the clean smell of his shirt, knowing that her tears were soaking through to his body. His lips gently pressed down on her forehead as he gently brushed back her wild afro and murmured assurances. She gripped him, wanting some of his strength to transfer into her but felt him tremble instead.

That brief tremble ignited a portion of her that had been too long dormant. Nicole felt a slow awakening throughout her body. It had been years since she had felt the yearning. She had thought that part of her was dead, but here she stood with her nipples sensitive and engorged as she pressed against Marty's chest.

Marty didn't immediately realize how this had so suddenly turned. One moment he was trying to soothe her anguish. The next, all he could think of is the way her body felt in his arms as the sobs went through her. His hand stroked her back, recognizing her missing bra and once that happened he couldn't help but feel her full breast as they pressed against his chest. Marty had always dealt with waif-like women whose body style was dictated by the media. He'd certainly thought they were beautiful even when he was alarmed that he could count their rib bones. But holding Nicole in his arms, with her full curves and toned athleticism caused him to become instantly aroused. He was ashamed that he wanted to move his hands under her shirt and to cup her breasts and cover her mouth with his...

Nicole buried her face into that space between Marty's neck and shoulder loving the delicious feel of his tender skin against her cheeks. He continued to shower her face and head with kisses, even while his breath came out in harsh gusts.

She yearned for him to kiss her lips; to feel his tongue and teeth and taste his soul. Nicole lifted her wet face to him and he stroked her tears away with gentle fingers...but he did not kiss her. Slowly she opened her eyes and stared at him. Marty.

Nicole jumped at what she was thinking, what she had just done. Quickly she slipped out of his arms, embarrassed at her actions. Why was she thinking like this? Before this week, she had never looked twice at the man. Now, it was all she could do to stop admiring his big tanned arms and his firm butt in his jeans. What was wrong with her?!

Marty moved to the stove. Quickly, while his back was turned, she reached for a paper napkin and swiped her face and discreetly blew her nose.

Without turning to look at her until his breathing returned to normal, he efficiently began gathering plates and silverware. "You have to be starving." His voice was light and casual even if he didn't completely feel that way. He picked up the skillet and with a spatula placed the delicious smelling concoction onto two plates.

Nicole felt the fire between her thighs begin to fizzle and die away to be replaced with confusion and anxiety. She tried to think of something light and flippant to say in response to his question, but her stomach betrayed her by grumbling loudly.

"I take that as a yes." He brought the two plates back to the bar and Nicole noticed that he kept his eyes averted, two red spots on his cheek as the only indication of what had happened. Nicole looked down shyly, only to see a monstrous omelet.

"Wow ... that looks delicious, Marty."

Marty dropped toast and then ladled up two big mugs of soup. "I hope you like tomato bisque." He placed one of the mugs in front of her.

"Yum." She nodded while looking into the mug of creamy goodness. "Is this canned or did you make this yourself?"

Marty's eyes finally met hers. "Canned soup?" The look of shock on his face was not manufactured. "In my home?" His voice was incredulous. "Never!" Then he smiled and any residual embarrassment between them melted away.

"Taste it," he said. And she didn't have to be asked twice.

"Mmmm. Delicious." He put toast on her plate and poured her an icy glass of tea then he sat down beside her and began eating, too.

Nicole glanced at him feeling a strange connection. He'd better be careful. She blinked. No. It was *she* that better be careful …

Nicole finished every morsel on her plate. "Very good." She said while leaning back in the chair.

"You *were* hungry."

She realized that she probably looked like a glutton. Truthfully, she had come from a place where if you were lucky enough to get a good meal then you ate it and remembered the times when there was no food … "Yeah. I'm not a small woman. I'm not one of those salad eaters." She stood and gathered their empty plates and bowls despite Marty's objections. She stacked them neatly in the sink.

"You say that as if you're a big woman, Nicole." Hell, she was…perfect, actually. He thought; who would be dumb enough to call Marilyn Monroe fat? Nicole stood at least 5'10" and she had full, heavy breasts, and he'd sneaked enough peeks at her backside to know that her ass was big enough to bounce when she hurried around the kitchen. Marty's felt his semi-aroused dick jerk back to life. Shit. He did not want that to happen.

Nicole humphed to herself. She was big and knew it. She was tall and big boned, athletic not exactly overweight. But she was big; big legs, big thighs and since having a child, big breasts.

Absently she set the skillet in the sink. She turned and looked at him, opened her mouth—and it was as if he knew she was going to ask him to take her home.

"Nicole … remember when you asked me why I'm doing this for you?" He took a deep breath and then walked into the living room. She followed curiously. He sat on the couch and she sat across from him in the armchair she had sat in earlier. He closed his eyes a moment and when he looked at her again it was in that detached way that she was most familiar with.

"Many years ago I was married, had a successful business and was living the American dream. One day my wife came to me and told me she was going to have a baby. I was so happy. Everything that I was working for was coming to fruition. Then she told me that it wasn't my child, that it was my partner's child. He also happened to be my best friend."

Nicole bit her lips and tried to remain silent. Marty continued to tell the story as if he was reading from a menu.

"In one day I lost my wife, child, best friend and my business. I decided that I wasn't going to let anything close to me again."

She looked away briefly, a familiar pang in her chest.

"I bought the restaurant, immersed myself in it … and refused to be dependent on anyone or anything. Seeing you at the door that night … " Marty swallowed and blinked his eyes. She saw the compassion return to them. "*This* is the Marty I was before. I can't turn my back now. Nicole, let me help you, just for the time being, just for a while."

She didn't believe that she had ever heard Marty talk so deeply about himself and his revelations brought back a lot of painful memories. Although the last thing that she wanted to do was to stay in her bosses house, she just could not see herself telling him no after all that he'd done for her and all that he'd gone through. Silently she nodded her head yes, hoping that she would not regret the decision.

Marty sat back and exhaled audibly but did not relax. "I … uh," He cleared his throat. " … don't want you to think that my intentions are…" he searched for the correct words. "Other then what I say." After all that he had revealed it surprised Nicole that he was turning red.

She felt her face turn warm again. No wonder Marty was so embarrassed. He was offering to help her despite the fact that she had just thrown herself at him. She was very ashamed. It was obvious that Marty's motives were pure. Besides, why would he want someone that was as broken as she was… broken in more ways then he would ever know? Silently, Nicole vowed to never again confuse her loneliness with desire.

She swallowed past her shame. "Thank you for everything that you told me, Marty," She sighed. "I'm not used to … relying on people or accepting help. It's always been just me. I've never had anyone to lean on. But at the same time, I am afraid that I might have another ... it might happen again and," She nodded. "So I'm going to say yes. Thank you. Yes."

Marty leaned towards her. "Consider my home your home. But, I am going to make one request."

Nicole raised her brow. "Of course, anything."

"This arrangement stays between us. I don't want the people at work knowing I have a soft heart."

She smiled. "No chance of that ever happening."

His response was just a slow grin. Her heart ached.

Chapter Eight

Marty took her on a quick tour of the condo. He had a state of the art home theater system and she wondered when did he ever find the time to enjoy the thing? But it was his den that she was particularly interested in. He had a computer. She didn't have one and going to the library to study and staying after class to research was a pain.

He had turned one of his spare bedrooms into a weight room and she understood now how he stayed so buff.

"There's only one bathroom up stairs." He apologized. "And I brought a few of your things. I swear I didn't go looking through your drawers — I just grabbed a few things."

Nicole shook her head. "That's fine. I could use my schoolbooks, though. I know I'm behind on my school work."

"I did pick up a backpack. It's in the den-" Nicole squealed and jumped up and down happily and then regretted it when her boobs swung loosely in Marty's oversized shirt. She pressed the sling against her chest and Marty pretended not to have noticed.

"Did you want to go back to the den and study?"

"No. I don't think I'd be able to absorb anything." They stood in the hallway silently. "Are you going to the restaurant?"

"No." Marty must have noted the flash of concern across her face. "I talked to Fred while you were resting. No major problems. He'll call me on my cell if anything comes up."

"I feel like I'm keeping you from work-"

"Don't be silly," he said dismissively. "Do you want to relax a bit, take a nap, watch a movie-?"

"Watch a movie!" She responded enthusiastically. Then she flushed, embarrassed. She didn't have a television. Yeah, she could have picked up a cheap one from Wal-Mart but didn't want to splurge on cable and really she didn't have time for television. But who could turn down an opportunity to watch a good movie on plasma screen with all the bells and whistles. "You have a real nice home theater."

Marty just smiled and gestured for her to follow him down the stairs. "Pick out a movie. I'm going to go pop us some popcorn."

Nicole's look of admiration was genuine. "Big screen, home theater AND popcorn? Man, I'll never leave." Marty's smile grew even wider.

Nicole examined the substantial movie collection and decided on the Sixth Sense. It had been years since she'd seen that one.

He returned with iced tea and microwave popcorn. "Good choice." He said when he put in the DVD. Then he sat down on the couch next to her. "Put up your feet if you want." He kicked off his shoes and got comfy. After a moment she slipped of her own and did the same.

Nicole had forgotten how spooky the movie could be and she caught herself jumping a couple of times. Marty laughed at her and she hit him with a pillow, completely forgetting that this was the boss that she had recently considered an asshole.

"Double Feature?" He suggested when the movie was over.

"Okay." She got up and scanned through his movie library again, stopping suddenly with a gasp. "No you don't!"

"No I don't, *what*?" He asked.

"No you do NOT have **THE PLAYERS CLUB** sitting in here!"

"I'll have you know that Bernie Mac played the hell out of that movie."

Nicole put her hands on her hips with a scowl. "Oh? So it wasn't the naked women?"

"Put in the movie, Nicole, and I bet you I can recite every one of Bernie Mac's lines." She put the movie in…and sure enough he did. Nicole laughed so hard that she had to hold her stitches. When Marty mimicked Bernie's line about white women not wanting to dance for the white man unless they got paid, and then Marty actually had the audacity to scream 'TITTIES AND ASSES,' Nicole literally cried.

"Marty, have you ever dated a black woman?" She asked when she finally wiped away the last tear.

Marty loved the sound and sight of her laughter. "No. But I've liked a few black women."

"Scared?"

60

He chuckled. "No. It just didn't happen, either I was involved or they were." His eyes lingered on hers. "What about you? You ever date a white guy?"

Nicole's brow furrowed that the script had gotten flipped. "Oh, um … yes." The look on Marty's face was priceless. He was shocked. "He was an Italian guy I knew a long time ago. Maybe you wouldn't call him *white*, but … "

"Who was he?" Marty leaned forward intrigued, wanting the entire story.

"Tomas … It was a long time ago." She didn't say anything else but Marty watched her intently willing her to continue. "I was twenty-one and I lived in … " She caught herself. "… an apartment that his Mom owned. She loved me." Nicole smiled in remembrance. "She fed me Italian food--real Italian food—not just pasta and marinara, but fish and scallops and stew. Did you know that? Italian food is more than just spaghetti and meatballs?"

Marty nodded smiling slightly. "What happened between you and Tomas?"

"Oh, I had to go home." Marty noticed that she was trying to hide her sudden discomfort. "My Mother died and I had to go home. I planned to go back to Italy but … things didn't turn out that way." She realized her slip and quickly met his eyes hoping he hadn't. No such luck.

"Nicole, you lived in Italy?" Again he was surprised.

She shrugged uninterested. "How did we start talking about me? What about these women?"

61

"What do you want to know?" He leaned back against his comfy couch and continued watching her.

"Tell me what they looked like?"

He smirked. "Are you asking me what I find attractive about black women?" She blushed. Yes, she was asking that.

"It's not in the color." That wasn't the complete truth. He always thought the contrast in color was enticing, however Marty had little interest in dark or light skinned. Nicole was caramel; neither dark nor light. But he would give his left nut just to see if her nipples colored pink or brown against her creamy flesh … "I liked two women who were black. I didn't like them *because* they were black."

"Okay. Point made."

He reached for the remote control and put the movie on pause and then he looked at her again. He was dying to ask her about Tomas, and about her living in Italy but knew that she was closed to the topic. He did have other things that interested him, though. "So now that you asked me, let me ask you. What attracts you to a man?"

The question caught her off guard. "What attracts me?" Flipped script again! "Wel l… I'm attracted to a man that's patient, kind, strong-"

"What about looks?" He was staring at her with those piercing grey eyes of his.

"Uh … Big guys. I'm a big woman. I have to be with a big guy." Quickly she clarified. "Uh … you know, muscular-" Shit! That had come out all wrong.

"Facial hair?"

"Yeah, I like facial hair."

"Long hair, short, shaved?"

"Shaved head is cool."

"Tats?"

She licked her lips. "I like tats."

"Piercings?" He shot back.

"It depends where."

"Where do *you* like them?"

"One ear only. No nipple or brow or facial piercings."

Marty stroked his goatee. "Are you hungry?"

"Huh?!" She jumped a little.

"Ready for dinner?"

He watched her innocently while she contemplated why she had just sat there and described the man that attracts her … and it turns out to be a description of him! She gave him a suspicious.

"Um, sure." She answered even though she wasn't hungry after the large lunch, and popcorn. It was just hard to look into his sexy grey eyes and not agree with everything he said. That conversation had been strange and slightly sexy which left a pleasant tingling between her thighs.

"What sounds good?" His voice was a slow sexy drawl. God, was he doing that on purpose? "We can do Indian, Chinese, Italian-"

"Indian?" She asked curiously.

"Do you like Indian?"

"I've never had it."

Marty's mouth curved in a slight grin. "Oh what sights I have to show you."

He had such a beautiful grin. Nicole found her eyes glued to his mouth. She jumped up. "I'll be back. I'm going to use the bathroom and take my medicine." More than anything she just needed to collect herself.

When Nicole was washing her hands she studied her reflection in the mirror. The soap began to dry on her hands as she took in the damage done to her. The sight of her face made her ill. Her eye was no longer closed but still swollen and discolored. Her bottom lip was split but healing with a crusty looking scab. Her normally luxurious curls were kinky and dry-looking. Her outside finally matched her insides ...

When she left the bathroom her mood was decidedly somber. Marty held up a menu, smiling. Then he noticed her expression and his smile faded.

"Nicole, what's wrong?"

She sat back down on the couch. "Nothing."

"Nicole?"

She touched her face. "I didn't know I ... looked so bad." She thought the scar on her lip might even be permanent.

"Baby Girl, you were just hit by a ca r... and you don't look bad." Marty rubbed his shaved head contemplating something and then he mumbled. "I think you're beautiful."

"What? You think I'm beautiful—you're nuts!" Even before the accident Nicole thought she was just okay—not beautiful.

"Okay ... I'm nuts, you're not beautiful, I just want to eat. Now can we decide on what's for dinner? I'm starving!"

Nicole chuckled slowly. This time it was Marty that looked at her suspiciously.

They decided on what to eat and Marty called the order in. He gave her a funny look.

What?" She asked touching her hair.

"Are you going to be okay while I pick this up? Or, why don't you com-"

"I'll be okay. I'll watch the rest of The Players Club. Just..." She looked around. It was starting to get dark. "Make sure all of the doors are locked?"

He picked up his keys. "Okay, I'll just be a sec."

Nicole turned the TV back on after he was gone. Then she sniffed under her arm. She could use a shower. She left the TV on and went upstairs. In her bag she found a denim button up dress that should be easy to get into and best of all bra and panties.

Nicole sat on the edge of the bed and took off the sling with just a little trouble.

She gasped at the stab of pain when she moved her arm. She tried to rotate her shoulder but it was still very sore. She had to pull her good arm and then her head through the shirt. Only then was she able to slide it off her bad arm.

She opened the bedroom door and peeped down the empty hall. She hurried to the bathroom, found spare towels in the closet, and then ran a steaming shower. It felt so good.

She examined the tape on her belly. She was going to have to change the dressing.

Nicole let the hot water beat onto her shoulder and it loosened enough for her to raise her arm midway. She washed quickly wanting to be dressed when Marty returned.

She dried off careful of her sore spots, wrapped the towel around herself and hurried back to the bedroom. She put on deodorant, slipped on her panties with no trouble, but struggled with the bra. Her hand was too weak to hold the clasp so that she could hook it.

"Shit!" She cursed and tossed the bra on the bed angrily. Nicole picked up the dress and carefully slipped it onto her bad arm. But once she got both arms through, she had another dilemma ... how to button. It was damned near impossible to keep the thing closed over her considerable bosom and to button it with one hand.

"Damnit!" She cursed again.

"Nicole?! You okay?" Marty was calling from the other side of the closed door and she saw the knob turning.

"Yeah! Hold on." She struggled to get the first button closed one handed.

"What's wrong?"

"Uh ... nothing. Hold on-"

"Why are you cursing if nothing's wrong? I'm coming in."

Marty opened the door just as Nicole clutched the dress closed in front. He appraised the situation and then frowned in annoyance.

Chapter Nine

"I can't believe you took a shower when no one was here." He stalked to her and she felt herself wanting to take a step back. But all he did was to kneel down to help button her dress from the bottom.

"Nicole, you could have slipped, blacked out..."

"You're treating me like a baby, Marty," she spoke quietly.

He looked up at her, pausing. "You can't even get your dress buttoned. You are somewhat helpless right now."

Nicole jerked away from him angrily, still clutching her dress closed in front. "But you don't have to talk to me like I'm a child!" She looked down and tried to button the rest of the dress, which meant her cleavage was popping out of the top of it.

After a moment Marty sighed. "I'm sorry. Let me help." He continued buttoning her up and Nicole refused to meet his eyes and he did the same. She noted his hands trembling slightly when he brought the material closed over her breasts.

Nicole stared at him surprised. He acted so calm and cool, and could flirt and put her on edge, but it was pretty obvious that he felt something being so close to her and now the tables were turned.

When Marty had her all buttoned up he turned to leave and something got to Nicole. She didn't know what exactly drove her to it, maybe it was because he had chastised her, or maybe it was just seeing his trembling hands excited her.

"Marty."

He turned, giving her a questioning look.

"Bandages. They got wet and need changing. I'd do it but … I'm so helpless."

His expression went apologetic. "Okay." He gathered the dressing for the bandages while she sat on the edge of the bed. Again he kneeled in front of her as she one by one undid the buttons starting at the middle and working her way up slowly.

He watched her, almost mesmerized until there was only one button left fastened at the top—straining to keep everything in. She lay down on her back which must have seemed like a very inviting position.

Marty audibly swallowed and spread the material to reveal the wet bandage. When he peeled the edge off the tape, Nicole braced her tummy.

"I'm sorry. It's probably going to hurt." He worked the tape away carefully and with much consideration. "Okay?" He peeked at her and she nodded. When the bandage was removed he gently applied salve.

"How does it look?" She asked, straining to see.

"It looks good. Healing good."

"Do you think it will leave a scar?"

Marty's eyes met hers. "Yes, but at least you'll be alive." He put fresh bandages on and carefully taped her up.

When Nicole sat up that last button at top finally popped loose and her breast spilled out of the dress.

Marty froze, his eyes glued to the sight of her beautiful breasts. They were full, what people paid thousands to get, she had naturally. And yes, her nipples were chocolate kisses against her caramel skin. Still kneeling in front of her, he reached up shakily. If there had been ropes tied around his wrists he still would not have been able to stop himself from doing it. Instead of closing her dress like he should have, Marty carefully placed both hands over her breasts.

Nicole caught her breath and felt an electrical charge between her thighs that matched the hardening of her nipples. She heard Marty groan as they tightened into hard peaks and prodded at his palms. He allowed his hands to softly stroke her breast, thumbs favoring the rigid brown aureoles and nipples. Nicole's eyes fluttered closed as she groaned, too. Her pussy was swelling from the almost forgotten sensation of being touched.

His dick had grown so hard so fast that it actually hurt! His dick had never ached like this before! He wanted to pull her legs up in the air and shove his dick into that beautiful pussy that he'd seen days before when he'd accidentally lifted her blankets.

He grabbed the material of her dress roughly and buttoned her closed. Then he met her confused eyes.

"I should have never done that." He shook his head and rose to his feet. "I'm sorry, Nicole. Let's just go downstairs and eat."

Nicole felt like someone had thrown a bucket of cold water at her. She had practically thrown herself at this man—and he had ended it. She could have buried her head under the pillow and hid for about a weak, but in the end all she could do was to nod silently, speechless, and then followed him downstairs.

Marty stormed down the stairs. He was so angry at himself. It hadn't even been one night and he was all over her! All he had to do was control himself while she was here, so that she could trust him and he could take care of her. That was all that he wanted and he could barely stop flirting!

It wasn't that he didn't have feelings for Nicole; real, legitimate, solid feelings. He just didn't want to confuse things. He didn't want a girl friend, a wife, and not even a lover that he had to work with her. That was just asking for trouble and he did NOT need to fuck where he worked. Why was he fucking this up?! He was attracted to her and obviously she was attracted to him. Did he need to keep poking at it??

When they got to the kitchen he silently spooned basmati rice, saag paneer and then curried chicken onto two plates. She watched him in painfully uncomfortable silence. He moved about the kitchen silently opening a foil wrapped flat bread that was still steaming. It was like a repeat of hours before when he avoided her look. She tried to think of something to say to remove the tension.

"Mmmm. That smells good." She went to the refrigerator and took out a pitcher of iced tea, filling their glasses as Marty took his seat, focusing on his plate of food. She sat down next to him.

"Chutney?" He asked.

"Who is that?"

Marty shot her a look then he burst out laughing.

"What is so funny?"

"Chutney is relish. Although it does sound like the name of a sixteen year old pop star."

Nicole grinned. "Shit." He spooned a sampling of three different chutneys onto her plate, still chuckling. She glanced at Marty and he was looking at her and just like that the two were again at ease.

The smell of the Indian food was foreign and she wasn't sure how she'd like it. But after her first tentative taste of the lightly spiced food she realized that it smelled stronger then it tasted. There was creaminess to the sauce that mellowed out the flavors.

"Oh," her eyes got wide. "I really like this." She mimicked the way Marty tore a piece of bread and used it to scoop up the food. Marty seemed pleased that she enjoyed it. He enjoyed watching her enjoy it. Down boy, he thought silently as his semi-erect dick began to twitch. It wasn't all about how much she turned him on. It was equally about just seeing her open up. She had been so closed to him for so long. He equated her to a blooming flower and regardless of anything else, just to see her like this was worth everything.

"Nicole, you're not wearing your sling."

Her arm was held close to her body. "Yeah … I've been able to move it more without it."

He nodded. She really didn't need him to go into over-protective mode right now.

Eventually, after some idle chatter and the enjoyment of a good meal, the sexual tension faded and the events

71

that happened upstairs were placed on the back burner. Marty grabbed his keys.

"Look, I'm going to head to the restaurant for a couple hours. I need to deposit some money and check on everything." He did need to do those things but he also wanted to clear his head. He sighed. "I'm not going to treat you like a baby — but don't do anything too strenuous like self surgery, acrobats-"

"Bye, Marty." She scowled.

"Nicole. Call me at the restaurant or on my cell," He quickly jotted the number on a pad by the telephone. "… if *anything* happens.

"Yes, Dad." She mocked.

He gave her a stern look. "And no parties young lady!" Then he slammed out the door. Once outside Marty took in a deep breath. He couldn't help but to shake his head at how much he enjoyed her company.

Nicole was chuckling to herself. God, why was that man single? He was incredible looking. She allowed herself the pleasure of reliving the feel of Marty's hands on her breast and the life returned to her core. It had been years since she had been touched like that. With a guilty sigh she pushed the thoughts away and went to the kitchen to do the dishes. It took three times as long as it should have but eventually she got them washed dried and put away.

She straightened the living room, put away the movies and turned on the television getting comfortable on the couch again. Before long she was asleep.

Chapter Ten

She felt something fuzzy against her face and opened her eyes alarmed. In her experience, something fuzzy touching you meant a rat had just scampered across your bed; whether that bed was a mattress or a pallet on the floor. Marty was covering her with an afghan and she relaxed.

"I didn't mean to wake you. You're a light sleeper."

She stretched and yawned. "What time is it?"

He sat down next to her. "Almost two."

"In the morning?"

"Yes."

"Marty! You've been up all day!"

"I don't sleep much." He explained with a nonchalant shrug. He seemed more concerned with her. "Are you going to sleep on this couch all night? You can if you want."

"No. I'm going to go up. How was everything at the restaurant?" She sat up and covered her mouth as she yawned again.

"Well, I had to make some changes. Kendall is doing your station and Fred has been doing mine. I'm going to go in tomorrow to help get her trained. When you wake up I won't be here. But I brought some food home from the restaurant so all you'll have to do is nuke it. I'm going to call you tomorrow so be sure to answer the phone when it rings, ok?"

"Okay." She stood up and rubbed her stiff arm. At least it was no longer sore. "Are you coming up?"

He pursed his lips and she realized how suggestive that sounded. "No. I need to unwind. I'm going to watch TV for a bit." Nicole went upstairs under his watchful eye.

"Goodnight." She called.

"Talk to you tomorrow."

She went to the restroom and then changed into an old t-shirt and a pair of athletic shorts. She didn't hear the hum of the TV so she figured he must be unwinding in the weight room or behind his computer. She climbed into bed marveling that his spare bed was a million times more comfortable then her real bed. Hers was just a lumpy pull out job that she got from a second hand store.

She sighed, feeling completely comfortable and at home. Her mind began to drift and to replay all the new things that she'd learned about her boss. Then, she remembered the way his hands had looked holding her breasts. His skin was tanned and reddened from work, but still pale against the brown of her breasts.

Nicole pressed her thighs together, feeling herself flame back to life. She didn't masturbate often because she found nothing to desire...but now, she imagined his lips closing over her nipples and her hand came up to stroke the hardened peaks. She sighed as her hips began to roll. She started to chuckle softly. This was all so strange. She was actually masturbating in Marty's bed, but the thought was so sexy!

Nicole's fingers slid between the heated folds of her lower lips and she was amazed to feel that she was already slick with her desire. She bit back a shuddered moan as her fingers began to work faster, her mind envisioning Marty doing things to her body that no man had done in years. Her voluntary celibacy seemed ridiculous when just touching herself brought so much pleasure. When she came, she muffled her cries into the pillow and spent a full minute trembling afterward. God what was that man doing to her?

Marty watched the ceiling of his bedroom. He hadn't been interested in watching TV and too tired to concentrate on book keeping, so had just come up to bed while Nicole was still in the bathroom.

Now his covers were pooled at his feet, his fist was gripping his swollen dick and he was mentally counting the number of soft sighs that were coming from Nicole's bedroom. He thought about lifting weights or taking a cold shower. But if he moved to get up then she'd know that he could hear everything she did…because she would hear him.

Damned vents that not only allowed for perfect eavesdropping, but amplification. His dick was too hard to ignore and he stroked himself in time to her breathing, imagining that he was pushing inside of her causing those sighs. Suddenly her sighs had changed into a low shuddering moan and Marty knew that she was cumming and he bit his lip hard enough to taste blood as he quickened his strokes. It took everything in him not to cause the bedsprings to squeak as he pumped rapidly into his closed fist. One low grunt was all that marked his orgasm, that and a fistful of creamy white cum.

He quietly pulled off his t-shirt and cleaned up. This is not good, this is not good, this is not good, he kept chanting in his mind. How am I going to do this?

Just as he said, Marty wasn't home when she woke up. The house felt empty without him. She went through the refrigerator and found a cornucopia! She nuked herself a ham, egg and cheese croissant and had a glass of O.J. and then went into the den to catch up on school work.

It was very hard to concentrate. Not only was she behind on her work, she also was having a hard time remembering the things that she had just been taught in school. Trying to remember only caused her to develop a headache so she cut off the computer and left the room. Call it forgetful or the accident but she realized that she was late on her medication. The instructions on the medicine bottle indicated that if a dose was missed to skip it and take it at the next regular interval so she did just that.

Nicole tried to watch TV but after about an hour, her head was pounding so bad that she couldn't stand the sound of it and the sun coming through the windows made it that much worse. She went upstairs to the bathroom for aspirin found it. Perfect. She took four.

She splashed her face with cold water, hoping that it would make her feel less nauseous, but when that didn't work she went back downstairs to nuke herself some hot tea. She was deciding between raspberry pomegranate and regular Lipton's when the phone began to ring. She hurried to the living room to answer it, feeling a bit disoriented.

"Hello." She said breathlessly.

"Hey, " Marty said. "What are you doing, running a marathon?"

"No." She sighed. "Nuking some hot tea."

"Why didn't you answer the phone?"

She scratched her head confused. "What? I did-"

"No. I didn't get an answer so I called back. I gave you about a minute, maybe two. How are you feeling?"

She was rubbing her head. "Um ... headache."

Marty didn't say anything.

"Marty?"

"I'm on my way home." He hung up. She looked at the receiver for a few moments before hanging it up and heading back to the kitchen to finish making her tea. Why was he coming home? Was he going to do that every time she complained about a freaking headache? She would have to convince him that she wasn't a delicate china doll. Nicole stared at the lukewarm water in her mug. It had just been steaming hot, now it was lukewarm. What the ... ?

Chapter Eleven

Nicole felt like she was being swung around in a circle like a kid on one of those playground torture devices. Gasping, she clutched at the nearest thing to her, which happened to be Marty. He was holding her in his arms a look of fear in his eyes.

"Marty?"

"You fell. When I came in you were lying on the floor." She reached up ignoring the straining in her shoulder and felt the back of her head. It didn't feel any more sore than normal.

"I'm taking you to the hospital." He said breathlessly as he hurried to the door.

"No."

"Nicole-"

"STOP!" He did, surprised. "Put me down." Reluctantly he did. "Marty, I didn't hit the back of my head."

"Let me see." He said, moving behind her and pulling aside sections of her afro. Tentatively he touched her head with his fingertips. "Maybe you didn't." He sighed and she decided not to tell him about the excruciating pain or he really would make her go to emergency.

"Nicole ... that's it." His eyes narrowed. "I am not leaving you alone again."

"Marty-"

He stalked away from her and walked back into the kitchen, picked up a fallen bar stool and angrily slammed it onto its legs. One minute she was risking a blackout in the shower, the next she was laying on the floor. Her head could have ...

Nicole just stood in the doorway because his attitude reminded her of the tomato incident, when he was so angry at her. But this wasn't her fault!

He glanced at her and then hesitated. "I'm not mad at you, Nicole ... but I am pissed. I am so mad at that lady that hit you! I am pissed that she left you there all alone." He raised his hands palm up. "And really, all I can think of doing is ... is-" He sat on the barstool silently feeling useless.

Nicole sat down next to him. "I understand." She realized that she finally did understand.

For the next few days Marty did stay close to Nicole. He took her to her doctor's appointment. He gave her his hands to squeeze when the Doctor removed the stitches from her scalp. He asked the pertinent questions about her seizures and blackouts and headaches and anything else he could think of. He made her healthy meals and even convinced her to go for walks around the neighborhood and eventually through the park. Donning sunglasses and a hat she was even persuaded to go out to a casual seafood restaurant that Marty loved. In the evenings they settled down to watch a movie on the home theater or she would do a few hours of schoolwork in his den.

Their routine was very comfortable and Nicole knew that she would never be able to see Marty the way she had prior to her accident. She wondered what it would be like once she went home and they had just a working relationship again. She'd miss him that was for sure.

Although they never discussed work or each other's past, she had grown to know him well, and he her. There was no more of the flirting but at times the sexual tension was nearly overwhelming. They both recognized that there was a mutual attraction. And they both knew that it was dangerous to play a flirting game.

By Tuesday morning Nicole's bruising had virtually disappeared and she was becoming anxious to get back to work. She glanced at Marty who was scrambling eggs wearing a pair of loose fitting athletic shorts and a worn t-shirt with the sleeves cut off. He had just finished working out and his muscles seemed very pumped. With a swallow, Nicole tried to suppress her rising desire.

"Marty." He raised a brow without answering. "Let's go to work today."

Silently he scooped the steaming eggs onto their plates. "Okay."

She smiled, "Really?" He put the skillet back on the stove then sat down next to her.

"Yeah ... But, Nicole. I think it's too soon for you to start working-"

"But-"

"Hear me out. It's just been a week since the accident. Three days ago you had a seizure. Let's see if you can go the rest of the week without one and I'll consider it. Deal?"

She hadn't had any other incidents since; no black outs, no seizures, not even a significant headache.

"I guess I can stay here and work on the computer-"

"I don't think so. There's a computer in my office at work." He hadn't been kidding when he swore never to leave her alone again. Even when she took a long bath he'd knock on the door after fifteen minutes or so to check on her.

Her sigh of frustration was real. "Marty, what's everyone going to think when they see me sitting in the office and not working?" Really, if he was intent on keeping their relationship secret then that would be a dead give-away!

"Even though I haven't told anyone that you're staying here with me, I'm sure they've figured out that I've not been around is because I'm with you. So tell them whatever you want. Tell them to mind their own business." He glanced at her. "But you would never say anything like that to anyone, Baby Girl. You're so sweet and nice." His tone was playfully mocking. She thought he'd be truly surprised to learn just how UN-nice she used to be.

"You don't care that they know you've been with me-short of them knowing that I'm staying here, of course?"

Marty's look was guarded, but he smiled. "No. Maybe they'll stop thinking I'm so mean. You think

81

that will change their opinion of me, Baby Girl?" He was always poking fun at her about the mean issue.

Nicole smiled. "You *are* awfully mean, Marty."

"I guess." He placed a mug in front of her then filled it with coffee. She was having a difficult time connecting this Marty with the Marty from work. She guessed that she'd see the other soon enough.

Chapter Twelve

Nicole kept sneaking looks at Marty as he drove them to the restaurant, trying to determine how he felt about this. He had turned on the radio to an oldies channel and was humming to an Eagles song. He didn't even seem concerned. Well why should he be concerned? No one was going to be bombarding him with questions concerning the nature of their relationship.

Nicole wasn't at the restaurant two hours before she began to regret her suggestion to come in, not that Marty would have let her stay home alone and she felt horrible keeping him away from work. But every time she began to get absorbed in her studies, the office door would pop open and someone would tell her how bad she looked.

When Kendall opened the door she was ready to scream, instead she just smiled. "Hey, Girlie."

Kendall's mouth just dropped. "Damn … "

"I look that bad?"

"No … but you do look like you got hit by an SUV. You okay, girl?"

Nicole shrugged. "A lot better than last week."

"Well I tried calling you but your phone just rang and rang." Kendall gave her a knowing look. She shut the door and sat on the corner of the cluttered desk. "Okay, Girl. Give up the goods."

"What goods?"

"The goods on Marty."

Nicole gave her an innocent look. "What in the world are you talking about?"

Kendall rolled her eyes. "Boyfriend closed the restaurant for you—for several days. Marty NEVER closes, not even when he had the flu!"

Nicole tried to appear nonchalant. "I don't have a driver's license. I guess I put Marty on the spot to help me out with Doctor's appointments, getting medicine … I feel real guilty about it."

Kendall just smiled. "Fred would have done any of that for you. I think he has a crush on you." Nicole scowled. She was so off the mark. "So … You don't think Marty sucks anymore?"

"I never said that he sucked! I just thought he was mean … But he's been real cool to me, so I won't complain."

Kendall stood. Nicole could tell that her interest in the conversation had expired and she had moved onto something different. "Marty is more than cool. He is the bomb!" She squealed.

Nicole frowned. "The bomb?"

"Yes! He's been training me. I don't know what it is Nicole, but he hasn't been his usual mean self … I think he wants me just as bad as I want him!"

Nicole was shocked but quickly concealed it. "Oh … really?"

"Oh my god! He's funny. He's sexy. And he watches me so hard. Girl, I'm going to get him!"

"Kendall, Isn't he old enough to be your father?"

"He's only thirty-nine or forty. That's not old. And besides he doesn't look it." She leaned closer to Nicole.

"I heard he's rich, used to have his own investment agency. He was married and everything. But she died, real horribly; killed-"

Nicole's brow furrowed sharply. "What? Kendall, how'd you find this out?"

"Fred told me. When Marty was out."

Fred? "How would he know about something like that?"

Kendall shrugged. "I don't know. I know that Fred quit another job to work for Marty when he first opened this place. Maybe they go way back."

Nicole felt sick. Fred wouldn't make up something like that. But why would Marty mislead her about his marriage because he sure made it seem like his wife had just dumped him for his partner.

Kendall looked at the clock. "I gotta get back on the floor. Nicole, what I told you has to stay between you and me."

She nodded absently. "Okay, but what do you mean she died horribly?"

"She was attacked, beaten, maybe even raped. I gotta go!" Kendall hurried out of the office.

Nicole shook her head in disbelief. Marty's wife was murdered? But why didn't he tell her? Maybe ... it was for the same reason that Nicole herself had never mentioned Alicia.

About an hour later Marty came in. "How's it going?"

She had been so absorbed in her studies and thoughts about Marty's wife that she jumped.

"Good, but I'm so behind on everything."

"Well, don't work too hard. How's your head? You don't have a headache, do you."

"No headache."

"Good. We'll cut out of here in about another hour, okay?"

She nodded. "How's Kendall working out?" She tried to keep her voice neutral.

"Real good."

"You know I'm coming back, Marty, and I want my job back."

He chuckled. "I'm not replacing you, Baby Girl. She's just filling in."

"I hope she knows that."

Another hour passed and Nicole needed to hit the restroom and to get something to take her medicine with. Fred was working Marty's station, it was pretty slow and he was working on a meatloaf. Kendall wasn't at her station and she didn't see Marty.

"Hey Baby Girl." Fred said looking up briefly. "You've been studying pretty hard in that office."

"Yeah, Fred. I got a lot to get caught up. Look at you, though. I hear you're the man with being in charge and all."

"You better recognize!" They both laughed.

She looked around. "Where's Marty and Kendall?"

"Getting stock." Nicole thought about how tedious getting stock had always been for her. Keeping the station replenished with fresh condiments, lunchmeats, salad makings and bread was time consuming. She decided to help, itching to do something a little physical.

"I'll catch you later Fred." She went into the walk-in, but didn't see anyone. The first part was the refrigeration unit, and then behind that was a second door, which led into a much smaller freezer unit. Rarely did she need anything from the freezer, most of her station was fresh. They must be out back getting carryout cups and trays. That could be pretty time consuming. She was about to leave when she heard a shuffle from the freezer. She opened the door and peeked her head inside.

Nicole's mouth fell open.

Marty had Kendall against a stack of boxes, their bodies pressed together intimately, her arms around his neck and his hands gripping her buttocks while his pelvis rotated sensually against her. They were kissing wildly, unaware that they were being watched.

Quickly Nicole let the door shut silently and then she backed away in shock. She stumbled over a box on the floor and silently stormed out of the walk-in. Her mind was crowded with so many emotions that she didn't know which one to process first, and then it became clear that the hurt took precedents over everything else. The hurt was sharp like a knife in her heart.

Nicole went back to the office allowing the door to slam behind her as the only acknowledgement to her anger. She turned on the computer and stabbed out the keyboard in order to save her work and to close out of the programs. Her mind kept going back to the sight of their hips grinding and she felt sick with the hurt.

To hell with it, she thought to herself angrily; humiliated. All this time she had thought Marty's reserve was based on his high moral: not to make a move on an employee and someone under his care. But obviously that wasn't the case. Obviously being employed by Marty didn't stop him from screwing you! How long had it been going on? Was it new?

Then it was true. The feelings she had were one sided. A tear slipped down her cheek and angrily she swiped it away. She was not going to cry—not over him, not when she had cried so many tears in her life.

Chapter Thirteen

Nicole wasn't surprised when the door swung open. She didn't look up from the computer as Marty stood silently in the doorway. Finally he cleared his throat.

"Were you just in the walk-in?"

Nicole looked at him briefly but didn't respond. She pulled a disk out of the computer and shoved it in her book bag.

Marty closed the door behind him and then rubbed his shaved head with both hands sighing. "I know what that must have looked like. But...it wasn't."

"Can we go?" She said, shoving the rest of her things in her book bag.

"Nicole ... "

"I'll be in the truck." She said, moving past him and out of the office. Nicole went out the back door and didn't say a word to anyone. Marty's truck was locked so she climbed into the bed and waited for him to come out, trembling, wanting to scream at him or smack him. But scream what? Smack him for what? Choosing the pretty white girl over the beat up black woman on public aid?

She eyed the nearby road wistfully. She wanted to be running down that road to her apartment! She wanted to be away from these people and their uncontrolled lust and then she choked back a cry.

In her entire life, all Nicole ever had was herself and then Alicia. She never grew up depending on anyone;

parents, friends and especially not a man. Her sole mission in life for the last couple of years had been to better her circumstances, not physical comfort—but to be a better person. Marty had been a brief interruption. But now, she was putting herself back on track!

By the time Marty returned to the truck she had herself under control again. Once she got her things she wanted nothing else from him. And she intended to play it cool because she wouldn't give him anymore than that. She jumped down from the flatbed and once he unlocked the door she climbed in before he could open her door. He watched her while he started the car and she knew he was dying to speak so she just turned on the radio and looked out the window. They drove in silence.

He pulled into the driveway but didn't cut off the engine.

"Nicole, Kendall is not who I want to be with-"

"Marty, I want to go home."

He swallowed, his shoulders sinking. "Okay … But Nicole-" She turned to him suddenly.

"Thank you for everything. I want to get my things, and after that will you just take me home?"

He stared at her seeing only a cold, blank expression on her face. He finally turned off the engine and handed her the keys. Wordlessly she went into the apartment and quickly gathered her things, ignoring the pang in her chest. There were a lot of good memories in this home. But she refused to humiliate herself anymore by thinking of them or of Marty. If Nicole was accomplished at anything, it was putting unwanted memories behind her. He was just a man that had done her a favor and that's all.

The drive to Nicole's apartment was quiet. Marty pulled into the parking lot but gripped her hand before she could jump out of the truck.

"Nicole, if you need anything, let me know. I mean it."

"Thanks." She said while pulling away, not even looking at him; in such a rush to be away from him that she practically ran to her apartment. He didn't even have time to get out and help her with her bags. She had them and was gone.

As soon as she had the door closed behind her Nicole began to shake. She leaned her back against the door and closed her eyes surprised to feel wetness there. She was just too disappointed to fight back the tears any longer.

Nicole had dumped the smelly items in her refrigerator and did the laundry before she even noticed that she had a number of telephone messages. Who would be calling her? She didn't have any friends anymore and her family was a joke.

She listened anxiously to the recorded voice of Mr. Rodriguez of District 12 Police. They had found the woman that had hit her, or rather she had found them. Apparently the poor lady had been looking for her.

After the accident she had been too frightened of moving Nicole so she had gone looking for a pay phone. Even after she had found the telephone she couldn't tell the police how to get to the site of the accident. When she finally got back to the accident site with the police Nicole and the bike were gone.

Officer Rodriguez had left the woman's phone number for Nicole to contact her concerning Insurance issues and instructed her on how to get back in touch with him in case she wanted to press charges. Nicole's heart lightened. That lady hadn't screwed her! The world wasn't full of fucked up people with fucked up agendas!

The last thing on Nicole's mind was pressing charges. After all, an accident was an accident. But if she could, maybe the insurance could get her bike replaced, and not to mention the out of pocket hospital and medicine expenses.

Nicole called Miss Westmoreland, the woman who had hit her, and she really was a nice motherly type. They exchanged insurance information and Miss Westmoreland insisted on paying for a new bike out of her own pocket. Nicole didn't feel comfortable with that, but trying to change the mind of a motherly-type with a guilty conscious was impossible so before they hung up, the two made a date to go out bike shopping the next morning.

That night when Nicole finally went to bed she was exhausted for the first time in a long while. The strain of seeing Kendall and Marty together not to mention the move made sleeping difficult. A big part of her wanted to quit her job so she'd never have to see either of the two again. But it had been a while since she'd gotten a decent paycheck and there was rent and living expenses to think about. Besides, the big reason she had chosen The Down Home Calabash was the flexibility in hours. She could get her forty hours a week spread evenly over the weekend. How many places allowed you to do that?

Eventually she fell into a restless sleep. She dreamt about the past, but it was Marty and not James that she was with. Alicia was with them and it was the way Nicole had always wished it could be ... Mommy, Daddy and Baby. She awakened the next morning with tears on her cheeks.

Miss Westmoreland picked her up bright and early the next morning and insisted on taking her out for a big breakfast and then they went to the sporting goods store. She replaced Nicole's mediocre bike with a state of the art European Tour-de-France racer. Nicole drew the line when Miss Westmoreland tried to purchase the matching helmet. Although it was out of her price range she bought it herself to appease her. They ended their day by stopping at the grocery store where Miss Westmoreland craftily paid for Nicole's purchases by mixing them with her own and paying for them on her credit card.

It made Nicole nostalgic for a mother. She had to wonder if this is the way a normal Mother would be. Nicole had never had one or been one. Her mind slipped back to the past and once more she could see the drug paraphernalia spread out on the cocktail table. James was nodding and Alicia ...

She picked up the telephone. She had one purpose and one purpose only, and that was to move ahead; even if she had to live in a crappy one-bedroom efficiency, even if she had to work with Marty and Kendall and their budding love affair.

Despite her resolve her palms began to sweat as the phone began to ring. She hated that she felt the least bit of nervousness at speaking to Marty. She refused to entertain that it wasn't nervousness but anticipation.

Chapter Fourteen

With relief she heard Fred's voice instead of Marty's.

"You know you don't need to come back so soon," he said.

"I feel better and I need to get back to work and school. What's the schedule like Friday?"

"Kendall was scheduled at your station. But she's here now. I'll let her know to either take the day off or do prep. Guess what?"

"What?"

"Marty made me manager. And I got a big-ass raise."

Nicole screamed and jumped up and down happily.

"It's about time!"

"Yeah, it was right on time. The dang fool went and broke his hand so he's out today."

Nicole felt an unwelcomed jolt. "Marty broke his hand? How?"

"You know Marty. He probably punched a wall or something."

"Alright Fred." She said, forcing thoughts of Marty out of her head. "Are you going to be in tomorrow?"

"I'm not supposed to be, but I'm like a doctor on call ..."

Nicole chuckled. "I hear ya. Well I'll talk to you later."

Friday evening Nicole strapped on her new helmet and tentatively sat on the bike. As she pedaled into the street she dry swallowed and realized that she was afraid. She looked at the busy traffic, heart hammering in her chest. With sweat pouring down her back she kept pace with the traffic. Her thighs burned a bit from a lack of exercise but after a few moments her confidence returned in small baby steps.

With the better bike she was at work in next to no time. She chained it out front and walked through the back door removing her helmet.

"Hey, Nicole."

"What's up Baby Girl?" She heard the familiar greetings and instantly felt at home. This restaurant was more than a job to Nicole; it was her family — her only family anymore.

Marty was grilling T-bones, some burgers, and making a deep fried catfish, expertly juggling each task even with the cast on his hand. He didn't raise his eyes once to greet her.

God he looked good, she thought. He was just wearing the same clothes he always wore; jeans and a t-shirt with the sleeves cut off. But somehow his arms looked bigger and the tattoo on his bicep stood out more. His shaved head gleamed still retaining the summers tan, smooth and newly shaved. Marty's goatee even looked ... better. And not to mention his muscled legs in the faded jeans ... booty looking like it should be pinched ... full lips looking like they should be kissed...

Nicole's cheeks felt suddenly warm. She inhaled slowly and approached her station.

Marty paused long enough to glance at her. "Baby Girl, I need two banana puddings." Although his tone was flat, the use of the nickname surprised her. At his house he called her Baby Girl, or Baby, all the time—but had never done it at work.

"Thank you." She replied and quickly plated the desert.

Fred gave her a quick hug. "You ready to take over?" She smiled and nodded. "Okay, then I'm outtie. Yo, Marty. Call me if you need me." Fred said as he headed out the back door. Marty just grunted some reply. It Looked like he was back to his old self.

"Nicole." Marty said. She turned to him, heart racing in expectation.

"Yes?"

"You're going to need to do some stock. We're almost out of ten inch lids and carryout trays. Also bring back some condiments; salt, pepper and ketchup. When you get back make salad dressing.

"Okay." He turned back to the grill and plated some burgers. She went out back to the shed a little hurt that he was so impersonal. Didn't he care how she felt anymore? He was setting the stage. It only made it easier for her to play the game.

The next few hours went just the same. He wasn't mean to her, nothing like that. But she couldn't stop remembering evenings on his oversized sofa watching movies and munching popcorn, laughing and going for walks...not to mention the feel of his rough hands again as they stroked her breasts. But, at the same time, she could still see him in the freezer kissing and moving his body intimately with Kendall in the way she had hoped-

With a grimace she closed the door on the memories of good times with Marty.

11:00 couldn't come soon enough. She hurried to leave bidding everyone goodnight. Marty was staring at her so hard that she hesitated; remembering how he had said that he didn't think it was safe for her to be riding her bike at night. But when he didn't speak she silently strapped on her helmet and left. Marty no longer had a say in her well-being.

Saturday dawned bright and sunshiny. Saturday and Sundays were her long days where she worked ten hours each. Monday was the only day a week that she had off and it made it very difficult for her to get as close to a forty hour work week as she could. Sometimes she didn't make it and had to juggle everything but the essential — schooling, which always came first. Eating, electricity, heat came last.

After taking a long hot bath she examined herself critically. The bruising had faded considerably. The cuts and scrapes were for the most part gone. Her shoulder no longer hurt when she raised it and other then some bruising still visible on her legs and thighs Nicole felt pretty well onto good-as-new.

She slipped on a pair of black jeans that she hadn't been able to fit into for months and then a sleeveless t-shirt. Even though it was fall you could count on it being hot in back.

She pulled on her bomber jacket and secured the helmet on her head. Then got on her bike and pedaled quickly to the restaurant. Her resolve was even stronger to put thoughts of her and Marty's past week together out of her mind. It was quite possible that he would be starting something with Kendall and if that was the case she had to ignore it—at least until she found a better job.

'Lord, just let me finish school. That's all. Then this nightmare can end.' She prayed. With one final thought she lowered her head before she pedaled off. 'Lord, I think I'm in love with him ... '

When Nicole got to work Kendall was already there and at Nicole's station. Awkwardly she walked up to her.

"Hey, what's going on?" Nicole asked in the way of a greeting.

Kendall gave her an up and down look before answering.

"Somebody needs to let me know where the hell I'm supposed to be working. The schedule had me on this station this weekend."

Marty flipped a sheet of bacon on to the grill. "That's not your station. That's Nicole's station. You're filling in for *her*."

With that said Nicole tied on an apron and moved on to check her stock. This wasn't her fight.

"Well what do you want me to do, Marty?" Kendall asked with an attitude.

Obviously she had forgotten who she was giving attitude to; King of the bad attitudes. Marty turned to her slowly.

"Kendall." Marty's voice was even but his look was heated. "Do cold prep." That's *your* station, isn't it?" Kendall huffed but retreated. Nicole just kept loading her station thinking the same thing that Marty was probably thinking; this is what happens when you screw your employees.

"How are you feeling?" He asked matter-of-factly. Well at least he was back to acknowledging her.

"Fine. Thanks." She responded politely.

He hesitated. "It's going to be a long day, Nicole. If you feel tired just let me know and you can go into the office and rest." He took in the sight of her faded bruises but instead of commenting on how good she was looking he turned and went to the walk-in, which happened to be where Kendall was. Nicole dismissed her curiosity although she couldn't completely rid her mind of an image of their previous refrigerator unit humping. She made herself an extra large coffee and hunkered down for a long day.

At 6 o'clock Marty sent her on break before the dinner rush. Unfortunately he sent Kendall on break as well.

Nicole didn't have much of an appetite but she ladled up a small bowl of chili and a large glass of iced tea. She sat down at the bar to talk to the waitresses and get caught up on gossip, which politely didn't include her.

Kendall suddenly appeared beside her with a plate of french fries. She sat down.

"Why didn't you say you were fucking Marty?" She asked in a casual voice. The front line waitress gasped and then there was almost a stampede as the others rushed to witness, what they assumed would be an impending fight.

Nicole's mouth dropped and she looked at Kendall in shock. "Kendall, are you out of your mind?!"

"Whatever." Kendall placed a french fry nonchalantly into her mouth. "I came to you and told you exactly where I stood, and you could have said something at that time."

She gave Kendall an amazed look. "Why would I tell your flighty ass anything significant about myself? Look at you; telling your business to the entire restaurant!"

Kendall's green eyes took on an evil glint. "Just back off, because you don't need to interfere with what we got going on."

"You truly are psycho." Nicole said as if she were seeing her for the first time. "This conversation is over. You do what you need to do, but keep me out of it because I haven't done anything to interfere in your life." Nicole stood up but Kendall wasn't finished.

"Then stay out of the walk-in when you know we're back there." Kendall's smile widened when Nicole's footsteps faltered. "You never know what you might see next time."

Nicole's blood began a slow boil. "Don't play those games with me, little girl. Instead of telling me, you need to be having this conversation with him!" Nicole knew that Kendall was trying to press her buttons, but despite this she could do nothing to stop herself from reacting.

Kendall smirked. "Oh I intend to tell him tonight when I see him after work." Though she never showed it on her face, Nicole felt as if a knife was being plunged into her stomach. Marty's home had been like her home for the past week and picturing the two of them snuggling on the oversized couch watching tv, kissing, touching...was sheer torture. I could kill this ho, she thought and that thought shook her.

"HEY!"

Everyone looked up. Marty was standing at the pass-through, a look of fury on his face. He had slammed his spatula onto the counter and now the entire restaurant was frozen.

Chapter Fifteen

"Both of you, BACKLINE!" He bellowed. If they hadn't had the attention of the customer's before – they had it now. The waitresses scattered and pretended to find something to occupy them. Kendall got up and headed to the back. Nicole watched her. As far as she was concerned she could just turn right around and walk right the hell out of the restaurant. And maybe she would even just tell the both of them to kiss her black ass! When her feet finally moved, she wasn't sure if it was going to lead her out the front door or not. In the end she followed behind the cocky young girl.

Marty was standing at the entrance of his office as the two women marched past him. She had never seen him so angry in her life. His face was past red and his eyes looked dark and dangerous. Even Kendall hesitated. He gestured for them to go inside. Nicole's head began to pound in suppressed rage. Neither would sit. Kendall crossed her arms and tapped her foot nervously. Nicole leaned against the wall and stared at the floor in front of her. She hadn't done anything wrong and had no intentions of being apologetic in order to appease his anger.

Marty closed the door and sat on the edge of his desk. He was quiet for what seemed like a long time before speaking. And then his voice didn't match the way his face looked.

"I'm sorry, both of you. I'm just going to say this." He sighed. "Nicole. I should have never led you on. I take full responsibility."

Still staring at the ground, Nicole did not see Kendall's grin. Her stomach plunged to the floor. This was really more then she had signed on for. It was one thing to have a secret crush on someone but for his new lover to flaunt over it was just much much more then she could bare.

Marty looked at Kendall next.

"And Kendall. I *never* led you on."

Kendall's smile faded. Nicole glanced at her in time to see that happen. But she only felt coldness. She didn't want to hear this. Whether Marty had feelings for the girl or not, she didn't want to listen to it, because he had already confirmed that he didn't have any for her…

"In that freezer, when you grabbed my dick, I told you that a man will only treat you like a whore for acting like that. But that was not my lesson to teach you. For that I apologize, Kendall." His face began to redden. It certainly hadn't had the desired effect. When he shoved her up against the wall and asked her if all she wanted was to be some man's slut and then he had roughly pinched her tits and pushed up on her, she had acted like that is exactly what she wanted.

"It's not even about being a slut or a whore." Kendall said. And for once her voice wasn't whiny, or faux sexy, or wannabe black girl. She just sounded like a twenty-five year old girl that wanted something that she couldn't have. "Why shouldn't I ask for what I want? If you want it too, then it's not wrong-"

"Because I told you that I didn't feel the same about you. You are a beautiful, smart girl that doesn't need to be some man's quick lay. What I did to you wasn't desire, it was anger. But you don't get that ... Still, I shouldn't have touched you and for that I'll deal with the consequences-"

Kendall rolled her eyes. "Whatever, Marty. Like you said, I grabbed your dick. So am I fired, or what?"

"Do you want to continue working here?"

She looked at him surprised. "Yeah."

"Then we can continue with my original plan. I'd like you to take over the cold bar during the days and you can work opposite Fred. I'll be working mainly nights working opposite Nicole."

Kendall squealed and jumped up and down clapping her hands happily.

"Thank you, Marty!" Nicole had not made a move or spoken once. Marty had cut back some of her hours but it was the only way that he could see it working. It would definitely keep the two women apart and it would keep her out of his way. And maybe it would give Fred something to occupy his attention so that he could stop trying to be the center of Nicole's.

"That comes with a raise, right, Marty?" She asked sweetly, as if she hadn't been completely scandalous just a few minutes before.

"Yes." He said blandly. He glanced at Nicole. "Kendall, go back out on the floor. Starting Monday you'll take over Fred's old schedule." Nicole turned to follow Kendall out.

"Nicole, wait."

She wouldn't look at him she was so mad and hurt that tears had sprouted in her eyes. "My breaks over. I need to get back on the floor-"

"I wanted to apologize to you-"

"I don't need an apology!" She said sharply. "Then I have to thank you again for taking mercy on me? Look, I already thanked you, what more do you want?" She glared at him, rage building in her with surprising speed, causing her to tremble.

Marty frowned, surprised. He was struck speechless by her reaction. What had he said to cause her to become so upset? He'd taken Kendall out of the picture ... was it Fred? He'd taken Fred out of her equation as well.

An angry tear fell down her face and she swiped it away quickly. "It made you feel good to help me and I needed the help so we're even. And for the record, you didn't lead me on. Because I never thought you wanted anything from me-" she raised a cold brow, "maybe something freaky but the opportunity you missed with me you took with her, so ... whatever." She turned to leave.

Swiftly Marty grabbed her arm and swung her toward him. He had a strong grip on her sore arm and although it hurt she didn't show it.

"Wait a minute!" He growled. "Didn't you hear what I said to Kendall? I wasn't trying for her. I'm ashamed of what I did to her but I wasn't trying for her!

And as far as freaky? Nicole, I missed a lot of opportunities with you because I *didn't* want that!" She tried to yank away but he held on to her tightly. "Furthermore, I *do* owe you an apology-"

"Will you let me go?" She asked in a chilly voice.

He didn't speak but his eyes grew equally as chilly. "No. Because I'm not done and you'll just run out of here."

"Just let me go and I'll listen."

He released his hold on her. "I'm sorry."

Nicole spun away and quickly pulled open the door. Marty reached past her and slammed it shut.

"This is crazy Nicole." His voice had lost its anger. She kept her back to him. "I really fucked this up. Nicole, please forgive me for everything that's happened. I honestly didn't mean for it to go this way." He stepped away from the door, allowing her the opportunity to retreat or to stay.

Nicole turned and looked at him curiously. "You fucked *what* up? What is *this*?"

Marty stared into her eyes. "I think I fucked it up between you and me." Despite her resolve to feel nothing, something leaped in her heart. Nonetheless she kept her face cool.

"Marty, what are you really trying to tell me? I'm not going to guess."

He had been trying to keep things between them on a friendly basis. The invisible line that he had set was supposed to protect his heart. But he was in denial; so much so, that even when she saw him kissing Kendall, he had tried to fool himself into believing that it would be for the best. He couldn't live with another heartbreak and he knew that he could be difficult. Why would anyone in their right mind want to deal with that? But one day without her was all that he needed to confirm what he was too stubborn to admit; he was in love with her and life was not worth living if he couldn't laugh with her, and talk to her, or just watch her when she didn't know she was being watched. This woman made him want to do better. And that meant that he could no longer go back to that empty life he'd had before she had become a part of it.

"Nicole, I want you to be in my life. I want to be with you. And," he shook his head. "… I'm not talking about sex I'm talking about loving you—all of you." She crossed her arms over her chest and felt her eyes grow moist. She blinked back the stinging tears and continued to watch him with the same angry expression. "Nicole, from the moment you walked into this restaurant I saw something in you that stood out from everyone else and it drew me. It continues to draw me. You continue to draw me."

Nicole's brow rose in surprise. From the moment she had walked into the restaurant? When he barely looked at her, or when he blurted out commands?

He tried to read her expression. "I know the face I show to you and the rest of the world. I didn't think I could ever want anybody close to me again. Today I can see how much of a prick I've been to the people I care about. I'm going to change that, Baby Girl." He whispered. "Even if you don't like me, I'm still going to make it up to you."

Another tear rolled down her cheek. And because of it she could no longer hold onto her anger.

Marty moved tentatively to her and she didn't retreat. Hesitantly he pulled her into his arms. Nicole sighed, relaxing the tension from her body. Marty sighed, feeling his fears fall behind him. They had both reached out in the only way they could, and despite how hard it had been to take that first step, they held on to each other now.

"I can't stand to see you in pain. Nicole, it just makes me crazy. I ... " Those tears in her eyes crushed him.

"Don't feel sorry for me-" she looked at him sharply.

His lips pressed against hers cutting off that statement as if he wanted to wipe it out of existence. Her body began to shake and she sighed against his lips. He opened his mouth and accepted it. Tentatively she touched her tongue to his and felt him shiver; a shiver that ran down to his toes. He closed his lips gently on her tongue capturing it and letting his lips glide sensually over it as he slowly pulled away. He had dreamed of his lips on hers for so long ... how those beautiful full lips would feel. And now he knew; it was like heaven.

Damn was all she could think. That hadn't been a kiss. That had been a landslide ...

Marty's eyes remained closed as he inhaled a deep breath. Then he looked at her carefully contemplating something. "I know this is not the right time to ask this but Nicole, I need to know something."

Nicole's eyes were dazed from the brief kiss. "Okay. What?" She replied perplexed at his serious tone.

"Where's your daughter? Alicia?" The question stunned her.

"How do you know about Alicia?" Her surprise cleared her head. Did child welfare contact him, or the court … the judge …?

"In the hospital you called for her. And your wallet had pictures of her..." She had to be hers. She was beautiful just like Nicole.

Nicole closed her eyes.

"My daughter is dead."

And before that very second she had never said those words out loud.

Marty groaned then stroked her arm tenderly. "I'm sorry, baby. I'm so sorry."

She waited for the familiar breaking of her heart. But this time it didn't happen, just the lingering regret.

He gave her a solemn look. "I'd like to hear about her one day. Will you tell me?"

Then she felt something too long locked inside slip away; much like a weight on her chest. She could suddenly breathe. For the first time in two years, Nicole could breathe. She'd never talked about her baby to anyone. She realized that she had been hoarding Alicia's memory—but also the pain; she had never released the pain.

Nicole slowly nodded her head. "Yes … I'd like to talk about her."

"I want to take you home; my home."

"Marty." She shook her head. "I can't keep taking from you. It's not my way."

"Nicole, I want to make love to you."

"Oh."

Chapter Sixteen

The drive to Marty's house was silent but not uncomfortable. She thought about the look of pure dislike on Kendall's face when they left together. Everybody looked at them. There was no more hiding what either of them was feeling, especially not after that argument. Marty's office was private, but when you're screaming at each other, that was not so private.

Marty pulled up into the driveway. Nicole looked at the familiar home. "I missed being here."

Marty watched her. "I missed you being here." They looked at each other and both got out of the car, Marty tossing her the keys while he wheeled her bike into the house.

Nicole slipped off her shoes and shrugged out of her jacket hanging it in the closet. It was like she had never left.

"Do you want something to drink?" He asked.

"No. I'm going to the restroom." Marty left for the kitchen while Nicole went up the stairs.

Her face was tear streaked. She splashed herself with cold water and it helped her to feel better. She smoothed a few stray strands of hair back, then opened the bathroom door and was about to go downstairs when she heard Marty speak from his bedroom.

"Nicole. In here."

She went into his bedroom. She had never been in there, though she'd passed it often. His room was very minimalist, but in a polished, very male way. He had a plush white rug over hardwood floors. The walls were painted a deep hunter's green and he had maroon accents that drew from an oversized abstract painting over the bed. The only other piece of furniture besides the bed was an armchair and a dresser. The bed wasn't even very big, maybe just full sized. Marty was sitting on it, expression serious. "Come here." He gestured for her to sit next to him and somehow the invitation wasn't at all sexy. Something was wrong.

"What's wrong, baby?"

He closed his eyes and sighed. "That sounds so good. Say it again."

Nicole smiled. "Baby ... "

"God, do you know how much I've wanted you?"

"How much?"

He cradled her face and kissed her urgently, restlessly. He stroked her hair, her back, sent his fingers gliding down her neck. He sucked her lips, teased her tongue. It was as if he couldn't get enough of her.

She couldn't breathe and it wasn't because he was there, it was because her heart was slamming in her chest and her limbs had grown weak.

She reached out and let her fingertips graze the length of him through his jeans. Marty moaned softly in the back of his throat. Then he stopped her hand.

"I have to tell you something."

She let out a breath. "Now? Because-"

"It's about my ex-wife. I have to tell you now before we go any further." She watched him silently, expectantly, his anguish seeping into her. He stood up and moved away from her, stroking his goatee and seemingly in deep thought.

"When my wife left me I remember wanting to punish her for what she'd done to us. I swore that I would never forgive her. I divorced her quickly, destroying all of her belongings." He paused becoming glazed eyed as he looked back to the past. "I got out of paying her alimony by threatening to smear her name. As for my partner, I sold my shares to our biggest competitor for half its worth." He looked at Nicole again. "As if that wasn't enough I went on a crusade to win her back so that I could dump her. I was consumed with hatred, all I could think of was ways in which I could hurt them; my ex-wife and my ex-best friend."

"She was probably in her 6th month of pregnancy when she finally conceded to leaving her lover to be with me again. I painted a pretty picture … and when she got to the house … " Marty swallowed stiffly," she had been roughed up by him." Marty looked down. Nicole covered his hand with hers. "I was supposed to run over to his house all enraged and kick his ass … Instead, I looked down my nose at her and told her that it was all a set up… and that she disgusted me. Then I made her go back to him; the man that had just beaten her." He looked at her then.

"It felt good Nicole. I didn't have one bit of remorse. The woman that I had at one time loved with all my heart, I now hated furiously. And I didn't regret a thing." He looked into the distance again.

"Well, the next day I got a call from my ex-wife's mother. My ex had been killed, beaten to death by ... her lover; my best friend."

Nicole gasped. "Oh my God, Marty."

He looked at her again. "He was furious at my crusade to destroy them and he was furious at her. He ... turned a gun on himself."

Nicole blinked in disbelief. Marty's eyes were shiny with unshed tears. She went to him but he turned away from her touch. Still she would not withdraw, placing her hand on his shoulder allowing him to know that she was still there. He shivered then turned back to look at her.

"I still loved her when I sent her away. God ... " he shook his head. "If I hadn't ... I sent a pregnant woman back to her abuser ... I hated her so much but yes, there was still love."

"Love and hate are two sides of the same coin." It was her turn to look into the distance. "We hurt the ones we love and it's the strangers that get our best. When you saw me after the accident it opened up all those memories of your wife, didn't it? Seeing me hurt?"

Marty stared at her, eyes still sparkling. He shook his head. "Seeing you hurt wasn't some Knight in shining armor syndrome. I just knew that I didn't want to turn my back on someone else that I cared for."

Nicole looked him deep in the eyes. "You never let me know that you felt that way. I had no idea."

"That was by design. Mean Marty was not letting anyone in." Briefly his expression appeared amused.

"It used to kill me when I'd see Fred and the guys hugging on you and calling you Baby Girl. I'd get so jealous.

She shook her head slowly. "Marty, I can't believe this … " he really hid it well.

"You really didn't know? I mean I couldn't help it sometimes when I'd be staring at your ass and … I thought it was so obvious. Every time you bent to clean that fridge it would take all of my resolve not to … " he just shook his head.

Nicole looked at him amazed. "Frankly, I thought you were an asshole." She scowled. "Remember the tomato incident?"

He half smiled. "Yeah. I remember there being two crates of tomatoes in the walk-in and you sent someone to the store to buy fifty dollars worth of puny hot houses. Did I ever tell you I hate hot houses? About as much as I hate canned soup." She felt her cheeks warm. He put his arm around her shoulder. He was grinning.

"I'm sorry I was an asshole." He kissed her lips lightly and her breath froze in her chest. She pulled back suddenly.

"Why did you curse out Fred that day? Was it because of me?"

"No." He looked surprised. "I was pissed at him…or maybe just pissed in general. But it was because of Mrs. Carpenter, or rather, Sister Carpenter; that poor old nun. She lives at the convent and she told me once that the food there is horrible. She once said to me that her one sin is coming in to the restaurant to eat, but only when she can afford it. You know, the nuns that live at the convent make very little money. I've once seen her pay her bill with change, down to the pennies ... I've tried giving her free meals but she won't take, what she calls charity. Imagine a nun refusing to take charity." He had a brief look of reflection on his face as he told the story. "But anyway, we kinda came up with a way to benefit both of us. I get to give her some good home cooking and she doesn't take a hand out." Marty looked at her. "So yeah, that's what that was about. But I told him about it and we got it cleared up."

Nicole didn't know what to say. "Well, why did she call him a 'boy?'"

His brow went up. "She's seventy. She calls me boy." He chuckled and then seeing her serious expression he ran his thumb tenderly over her knuckles.

"Baby, Fred and I are good."

"Ok." She whispered, staring deeply into his grey eyes.

"Ok." He repeated. "And you and Fred. How good are you two?"

Nicole reflected on how long she'd had to stew, contemplating the nature of the relationship between Marty and Kendall. Well she wouldn't be mean and make him suffer as she had, but she did intended to give him a teeny bit of payback.

"Oh Fred is great. He's probably my best friend." Marty looked crushed. "I mean, when I need a friend sometimes he's the only person I have to turn to." Which wasn't a lie. He was the only person that she could call 'friend'.

Marty looked into her eyes so deeply that she could see his eyes tracking every movement of hers. Damn, she had never been looked at that hard. She decided to come clean.

"He is a great guy. I'm sure his boyfriend appreciates his friendship as much as I do."

His eyes widened. "His what?" He suddenly smiled. "You're evil."

She laughed until she fell back on his bed and then she stuck out her tongue at him.

He just froze. "Damn that's sexy ... " he kissed her again, quicker, more passionately then he had before, his bare arms on either side of her, supporting his body above hers. She ran her hands up his body, not believing the hardness of his muscles beneath his loose fitting t-shirt. She could not believe that she was touching the body that she had admired for so long. He was perfect. He was hard and sculptured without being hulking. Nicole felt herself begin to throb erotically.

But there was something she had to do. Because he had been brave, she would be as well. So instead of enjoying his kiss, she placed her hands flat against his chest and gently pushed him away. Slipping from beneath him, she slowly walked across the room.

"What's wrong? Am I moving too fast?"

"No, that's not it." She turned to him and there was a look of pain deep in her eyes. "Now it's my turn to tell you something ... and it's not a pretty story."

Chapter Seventeen

Marty stood, pulling her into his arms. "Baby, I told you the most horrible story about myself and you listened without judgment. You don't have to do this now. There is nothing that you can tell me that will affect how I feel about you-"

"But I have to tell it for me."

Reluctantly Marty released her. He sat back down on the bed. "If it's that important to you, I'll listen to whatever you need me to hear."

Nicole stared at an invisible spot on the carpet. This wasn't a story that she could tell and look Marty in the face with the telling of it.

"I grew up in the projects ... I guess you'd call it the ghetto. My life ... wasn't good. My mother was single. She had five kids—that lived. We all had different fathers and my own Daddy had twelve kids—at last count. None of my brothers and sisters were close. We all had different Daddies and so, for the most part, a lot of my siblings would be off with other relatives that I didn't even know. Actually, my youngest sister; I've only seen her a few times in my life. She lived with her Dad's family so really my Mama was all I had. And I loved her; don't get me wrong by what I've just said. I loved my Mama with every breath of my body." She sighed. "I guess my world revolved around her. She was... God, as far as I was concerned." She remembered something that she had he ard from a

movie once; to a child mother is the word closest to God
...

Nicole cleared her throat as she recounted the events of her life. She didn't see the carpet that she was looking at, but the linoleum floor of their townhouse home; the one that she'd had to get down on her hands and knees once a week in order to scrub the old wax off before another sibling put the new wax on.

"We were on welfare so I never had much." She turned to look at him reluctantly. "Welfare was all I knew. I figured I'd grow up, have kids and be on welfare, too. Then there was school, which I was horrible in. I got held back in 9th grade twice, then I just quit." Marty looked at her surprised. "Once I dropped out I just hung out with friends, smoked dope ... nothing too hard. James, my boyfriend got me a little job at the stadium. He was much older than me; actually he was a grown man. I was just sixteen.

"The Stadium was the best thing that ever happened to me. It wasn't the ghetto and I got to see the other side—life outside of the projects." She was finally brave enough to meet his eyes.

"I guess seeing different people with nice things made me decide that I wanted more, so I joined the Job Corps. I got my GED high school equivalency and then went to trade school. I received certification in accounting, childcare and computers. I was there for two years but I couldn't seem to learn enough. I was like a sponge and I wanted to know more. I also liked the structure so I decided to join the Army."

When Marty raised a surprised brow, Nicole just nodded and smiled briefly. "I fulfilled my two years and stayed for another two. I probably would have been a lifer. I have a bachelor's in communications and was just a few months shy of my masters in computer programming when I received news that my Mother had died."

"*Ho vissuto in un piccolo appartamento fuori di Napoli.*" She said in fluent Italian. "That means; I lived in a small apartment in Napoli … and that's about all the Italian I can remember." She smiled briefly and Marty did too, knowing that he could never have figured out this side of this amazing woman on his own. He just knew that he admired her even more than ever that she'd been able to pull herself out off the hell she'd been living.

"In Italy I made real friends for the first time in my life. I lived in this little apartment owned by this chubby little Italian woman who wanted to marry me off to one of her sons." She had a reflective smile on her face. "Tomas was the youngest and he was unlike anyone I'd ever met before. He thought I was a goddess." She chuckled.

Marty knew that he should probably be jealous of this Tomas, but he also knew that she needed someone to see the beauty in her and therefore he was happy that he had been there to show her.

"But then I got the call about my mother." She had promised them that she'd return, but had never even called. "When I got home I saw that nothing had changed there. I had. But everything there was just the same, even that fucking linoleum floor that I'd had to scrub once a week since I was nine years old. You have to understand, Marty. My Mother was my life in the projects. I mean, she was hard on us. You could call it abusive. But I loved her. Being back there without her made me feel isolated; alone. It made me want to seek out my family connections again which, in my case, had been the streets.

"I discharged from the Army and got an apartment and a decent job in an office. But I was back to hanging out with my friends on the street, smoking dope...and now I could afford the harder stuff." Nicole closed her eyes and when she opened them again she stared into the distance. "I started using heroin, and coke. James; my old boyfriend, and I got back together. Before I knew it I was pregnant.

"For a hot second I got some sense and kicked James to the curb and stopped doing dope." She shook her head angrily. "But then my job let me go because I was pregnant."

"What? But that's illegal."

"Yes, but they did it in a way that made it appear that they were just downsizing. I was last hired so I was first fired.

"It killed me to do it, but I couldn't find another job so late in my pregnancy. So...I had to get on welfare." Nicole swallowed. "I really worked hard so that I would never have to resort to that life. But with all of my training in the workforce, still a pregnant 25 year old black woman was no big catch." Marty looked at his feet silently.

"I was alone so...back came James. But I didn't use, not while I was pregnant; never when I was pregnant." Marty didn't look up. Nicole took a deep breath and despite her resolve, felt her eyes sting. "Alicia was born and...she was so beautiful. She looked like a little Angel. Everybody told me to get her into modeling or movies. I jus t... " Nicole paused. "I found myself a little job when she was a couple months old. But there was no way, Marty, no way that I could afford a place out of the projects, daycare and a baby on that salary. So I let James back in my life with dreams that we'd get married and be a family. Together we could make it. Well ... he didn't share my vision.

"So there I was. Two degrees and living in the fucking projects on fucking welfare! What people don't always realize is that you can be on assistance and still work. You can get vouchers for your child for food, medical, even daycare. And obviously it's reduced the higher paying job you have. So someone like me that finds a good job, but has to work their way up, can't afford all-day daycare for a newborn baby, an apartment, and food...one of those things has to go. Hell I'm not even talking about phone, bus fare, cable, I'm talking the essentials." She sighed again. She was here to tell the story, not to apologize, not to appear like a villain or a hero. She continued. "I went back to hanging out with my old friends and getting high." Tears dropped from her eyes but her voice never changed and Marty never looked up.

"I thought ... I convinced myself that I was keeping it under control when I only got high after Alicia went to bed. But then the crave started hitting me during the day and I'd take Alicia to a neighbor's house for a couple hours while James and I got high. Then it was; put her in her bed or play pen and go get high. And then after a while it was; 'she's two. She doesn't know what she's seeing.'" Her voice broke and she swallowed back tears.

"James came over with some crack cocaine one day. I'd just made Alicia lunch and she was in her high chair watching her favorite cartoon show on TV. Well ... " She gulped. Tears dropping like fat raindrops. "James and I started smoking, sitting on the couch, watching cartoons with Alicia." She still remembered the song playing in the background and Alicia's tiny voice singing along '...if all the raindrops where lemon drops and gum drops oh what a rain it would be; standing outside with my mouth opened wide ... ' "I remember coming fully awake. Alicia wasn't in the highchair. James was still there nodding. Every time before, she'd be in front of the TV, even if she did manage to climb out of the highchair." Nicole sniffed down more of the tears and continued in a hoarse voice, drops dripping from her chin and splashing her shirt.

"This time, though, Alicia was lying on the floor with...with crack rocks falling out of her mouth. I screamed, picked her up and ran to one of my neighbors. You see, I was so fucked up I didn't even think to call 911. My baby hung on for two days ... " Nicole defiantly swiped her wet face while Marty refused to look at her.

"My charge somehow was reduced to child endangerment and I got two years probation. I never asked for it, didn't care at that point and to this day can't remember how and why it happened. James got eighteen months in prison for brining the drugs into the house. When the Judge looked at me, I saw in her eyes such contempt. She told me that what made my case so bad was that I **did** have an education … that this was a choice I had made. I don't remember any of the events around that time but what that judge said to me will forever be seared in my brain. That was the very second I died. And the person that walked out of that courtroom was not the same person that walked in. No handcuffs, no jail sentence … but I was better off dead. The judge hadn't lied. That had been my choice."

Marty looked at her then. Tears dropped from his eyes, too. "Nicole, I am so sorry, baby … " she looked down at her hands.

"Although they didn't set a punishment for me, I set my own … it was more a goal. I must finish my schooling, have a career and have a home. Until I've done that my life is not my own. Then I'm going to write that Judge and tell her that Alicia didn't die in vain.

"That's why I don't have a car and I live in a shabby little apartment and school is my life. That's why … "

"Why you can't accept help?" Marty said solemnly.

"I don't quite know who I am. The person here now is no one I ever knew before. I'm not the girl who lived in the projects or Alicia's mother. I'm kind of …

nothing; just a person trying to facilitate an ends to a means."

Marty stood slowly. "I had no idea." He pulled her into his arms. Nicole was amazed that he could stand to touch her after what she'd just told him. Gratefully, she allowed it. The door to Alicia was cracked open finally.

"Nicole. I want you to hear me." He was holding her tight. "I'm not going to ask you to lean on me. I'm going to ask you to let *me* lean on *you*." A small sob escaped her. "At first I thought it was me that was helping you, but now I know that it's just the opposite. I need you. I need you."

Nicole raised her arms and wrapped them around Marty's neck.

"You feel this way even after the horrible story I told you?" She asked, face hidden in his neck.

He pulled back and looked deeply into her worried eyes. "I want to be with you. That's all I care about." This time when he kissed her it was gentle and reassuring. She became liquid in his arms.

"Nicole," he croaked, pulling back from her.

"Yes, Baby?" She responded eyes hooded.

"You're fired."

"What?" Her arms dropped away from him and she stepped back confused. "Are you joking?"

Marty's eyes were apologetic. "I'm sorry, Nicole. I can't have a personal relationship with one of my employees-"

Nicole's mouth dropped in disbelief. "You're serious?"

"If I worked that closely with my girlfriend, then it would be chaos-"

"You're going to fire me?! You could just work days-"

"But then I'd never see you-"

"Well FUCK that!"

"I know of another job-"

"Oh my God ... " She turned away from him and began to pace. "Oh my God, you are such an asshole. After what I told you and how important it is for me to work-"

He tried to touch her but she side-stepped him. "Baby girl, hear me out. I know-"

"Will you reconsider what you just said?" She asked simply. He was already shaking his head.

"I can't do that, Baby. No, but-"

He heard her chuckle. "Well what if I don't want to be your girlfriend?" His face paled. "But I do." She said softly. His breath came out in a rush of relief and in one quick motion she pulled off her shirt, than unhooked her bra. Marty's eyes moved from her eyes to her breast where they lingered — then back to her eyes. What was she doing?

Nicole placed her hands on his chest where she lightly pushed him back until he fell back into a sitting position onto his bed. He didn't know what to do. One minute she was spitting fire, and the next she seemed to be controlled by desire. She knelt down on her knees, positioning her body between his knees. She ran her hands up his thighs and his muscles tensed slightly.

"Take that off." She commanded while tugging at his shirt. He quickly swept it off. Her fingers slid to his crotch and Marty's exhale was audible. She slowly unzipped him, slipping her hand boldly into his shorts where she pulled out his rapidly hardening cock.

Marty gasped in surprise. Nicole eyed what she held in her hands hungrily. Then her eyes met his and Marty leaned back on his elbows and decided to just watch.

Gently, Nicole stroked the shaft, her eyes never leaving his. She leaned forward and her tongue snaked out and flicked the head of his cock.

"Oh God ... " He groaned.

Nicole's tongue traced a circle around and around the sensitive head.

"Fuck!" Marty gripped the sheets blinking rapidly.

She placed her lips around him before sliding her mouth down his shaft until he had pushed down her throat.

"Fuck fuck fuck fuck fuck!" Marty threw his head back in ecstasy.

Nicole reached down with her left hand and lifted her breast. She removed her mouth from Marty's cock long enough to snake out her long tongue and flick it around and around her taut brown nipple. She looked at Marty wide-eyed.

His mouth parted slightly. "Shit ... " He whispered.

"Marty?" She purred in a deep sexy voice. "Can I have my job back?"

He was nodding before she finished the sentence.

She slipped his cock into her mouth as deeply as she could.

"Fuck!" He yelled.

Delicately she removed it from her mouth, "Baby? Can I have a raise?"

"YES!"

She wrapped her lips around him once again. Marty suddenly tensed, the orgasm hitting him by surprise. Nicole gripped his cock and watched him spurt clear into the air, a small grunt broadcasting each spurt of semen. It was like cannon fire! She let the mess gather on his tummy and she used her forefinger to trace along the warm creamy fluid while his muscles twitched involuntarily at her touch.

He lay back on his the bed in exhaustion and Nicole took his discarded shirt and wiped him clean. She then joined him, on her belly, kissing his lips and chin and nose.

Marty reached up his hands holding the back of her head while he kissed her deeply, taking her breath away. Effortlessly he changed positions with her leaving him on top. Again, he kissed her lips, her chin, her neck. His tongue snaked out, equally as long as hers and he trailed it down her breast and over her nipple.

Nicole squirmed at bit, her pussy throbbing and pounding mercilessly.

Marty pushed both breast together and then alternately licked and teased one nipple then the other. He watched her reaction intently.

"Oh...damn." She groaned, her eyes hooding slightly. He released one breast fingering the nipple while he sucked the other. Gasping, Nicole rotated her pelvis against his thigh.

Marty suddenly lowered his attention and knelt between her legs. He hooked his thumb into her jeans and pulled them off.

Marty couldn't take his eyes from the mound of dark curls. With two fingers he gently stroked her slit, finding that she was wet and steaming hot. He looked up at her while he continued stroking with his fingers. Nicole's eyes were two sexy slits. She gyrated her hips in time to his manipulations. He spread her lips and pressed his mouth onto her hot pussy.

"Ohhh!" She gasped, hips jerking involuntarily. Marty's tongue rapidly jack hammered against her sensitive clit. This he alternated between long slurpy licks, continuously gauging her reaction, barely taking his eyes from hers. Nicole threw her head from side to side.

"Oh … shit!" She groaned.

"Is that the spot, Baby?" He mumbled between mouthfuls of pussy.

"Oh yes, Baby … " she cried deliriously. "You do that so goddamn good!"

His tongue slipped into her as far as he could reach, pushing until the thickness was fucking her. Nicole's legs spread further and she gripped his head holding it in place.

Deep inside of her he began the jack hammering.

"Oh ... FUCK!" She yelled. Marty moaned and continued to beat into her pussy, her hips pumping into his face. "FUCK ... " she yelled. Quickly he pulled his tongue out of her and hammered her clit, all the while never removing his eyes from her face.

"Do you want my cock now?"

Nicole gripped his bicep. "Yes, oh YES!"

Marty positioned himself above her, cock heavy and bobbing. Nicole squirmed anxiously.

He stroked himself a few times watching her watch his cock. His lip curled into a brief smile of pleasure.

"Baby Girl?"

"Uhm ... what, Baby?" She moaned watching the motion of his hand. Marty bit his lip as he increased the speed of his stroke.

"When you come back to work ... " he sucked in his breath involuntarily at the sharp build up of pressure. He placed the head of his cock against her nether lips. Teasing he slipped it slowly into her tight opening.

"Oh! God ... " she thrust upward.

"Will you give me two weeks notice?"

"Oh fuck ... Baby." She thrust upwards again.

Marty withdrew a bit. "Two weeks notice, Baby?" He plunged his cock into her completely and she sucked her voice audibly. He pulled back out almost completely and waited for her response. Nicole stared between them at his oversized cock poised for another re-entry.

"Yes, Baby!"

"Say it." He plunged his cock into her once more but instead of withdrawing rubbed his pelvis against her enticingly.

"Oh shit! Okay! I'll give you two weeks notice! Now stop teasing and make me cum! PLEEEEASE!"

Marty planted his arms on either side of her and pumped his cock in and out of her rapidly.

Nicole's insides tensed and before she knew it a volcano erupted. She threw her head back against the bed while the orgasm overtook her. Her mouth opened and she called out Marty's name in a wild voice. Over and over she moaned as he worked his cock in and out of her until she was nothing more than a bundle of nerves. She froze and shuddered with an aftershock.

"Shit." She moaned softly. She wrapped her arms around Marty as he withdrew his still erect cock from her and lay on top of her body carefully.

"You fired me again." She said half accusingly, half amused that he had flipped the script on her.

"You're quitting." He mumbled into her neck, sleepily. "Or else we're going to end up fucking in the shed, in the office, in the walk-in…on the counter. I know this, especially after what you just did to me." He rolled off of her gently and pulled her into a spoon position, cupping her breast. "Gee, I wish I knew where I could find a good personal accountant. Say, you took accounting in Job Corps. Maybe you know of someone that you could recommend to keep my books?"

She turned and looked at him in surprise. So that's what he meant; another job, one where they wouldn't have to work together. She smiled. "Yes, but she'd need a raise."

Marty chuckled. "Oh, I got a raise for you … "

~Epilogue~
TWO YEARS LATER

Nicole pulled into the driveway of an old but beautiful Victorian house. Just like she always did, Nicole paused before getting out of her car to admire the beauty of the old trees and the wrap-around porch. She loved everything about her house; every leaky pike, every drafty window just as much as she loved the nine foot high ceilings, hardwood floors and oversized kitchen.

She grabbed her briefcase and locked the door to the CAMRY still getting a kick out of the little twerp, twerp sound the security system made when engaged. She'd had the car a year but still got a kick out of little things like that.

She hurried to the house, careful not to allow her pumps to sink into the mud. The landscapers were far from finished with the yard. She just hoped they would be finished before the snow fell. She wanted her first Christmas in her first home to be picture perfect. Absently she brushed a bit of lint from her Dolce and Gabbana suit, and then unlocked the front door.

Santana was playing from the stereo and the smell of something delicious was in the air.

Nicole placed her briefcase on the side table.

I'm home." She called. "Where are my boys?"

Marty came out of the kitchen with the baby carrier strapped to his front.

"Hi, Baby." He kissed her. "How was work?"

"Ahh ... " She said exasperated. "I'm going to be working on that project this weekend." She gently pulled her snoozing son out of the carrier. He was a plump four month old with a head just as bald as his Dad's shaved one, hazel eyes also like his Dad's, and the caramel skin of his mother. "I don't want this project interfering with our plans to spend the week with your parent's."

"I know. They've only seen M.J. twice." Marty unstrapped the carrier and tossed it on the couch. "You hungry, Baby? I made a veal scaloppini."

"Yum. "I'm starving." He pulled her into his arms, their son cradled carefully between them. He kissed her more intimately.

M.J. reached up and grabbed his Dad's chin cooing playfully. He took him out of Nicole's arms.

"Okay, Junior. Come to Daddy. Let's allow Mommy to get changed for dinner."

"I'll be right back." She hurried up stairs to change. Marty put M.J. in his playpen. M.J. gave his Dad a speculative look and then found his feet to be of interest and began to place his toes into his mouth. Marty leaned over the playpen and stared at his gurgling boy.

"Wow, son. That's really something. Good job." He was in constant amazement at this little boy that he and his wife's lovemaking had created. He was beautiful.

Marty shook his head chuckling and then he went into the den and put the finishing touches on the letter he had been writing.

.....five years ago my wife lost her daughter, and that in itself caused her to shed her former self. No longer is she the drug addicted single mother living on welfare in the projects. She has cut herself free of the net that most of us never recognize is just a trap designed to hold one down. I'm proud to say that my wife flipped it and made the system work for her; allowing her to complete her degree in computer programming. She is now the managing director of an up and coming Internet Web design company. When my wife's mission ended, she put her past behind her. But I'm here to complete her final task; which was to let the Judge that heard her case know that Alicia did not die in vain. My wife has a successful career, a number of degrees, a beautiful Victorian house, and...more importantly, a husband and baby son that adore her...

THE END

PEPPER PACE BOOKS

~~***~~

STRANDED!
Juicy
Love Intertwined Vol. 1
Love Intertwined Vol. 2
Urban Vampire; The Turning
Urban Vampire; Creature of the Night
Urban Vampire; The Return of Alexis
Wheels of Steel Book 1
Wheels of Steel Book 2
Wheels of Steel Book 3
Angel Over My Shoulder
CRASH
Miscegenist Sabishii
They Say Love Is Blind
Beast
A Seal Upon Your Heart
Everything is Everything Book 1
Adaptation

SHORT STORIES

~~***~~

Someone to Love
MILF
Blair and the Emoboy
A Wrong Turn Towards Love
The Delicate Sadness

~~***~~

Baby Girl and the Mean Boss

COLLABORATIONS
~~***~~

Seduction: An Interracial Romance Anthology Vol.
1
Scandalous Heroes Box set

About the Author

Pepper Pace creates a unique brand of Interracial/multicultural erotic romance. While her stories span the gamut from humorous to heartfelt, the common theme is crossing racial boundaries.

The author is comfortable in dealing with situations that are often times considered taboo. Readers find themselves questioning their own sense of right and wrong, attraction and desire. The author believes that an erotic romance should first begin with romance and only then does she offers a look behind the closed doors to the passion.

Pepper Pace lives in Cincinnati, Ohio where many of her stories take place. She writes in the genres of science fiction, youth, horror, urban lit and poetry. She is a member of several online role-playing groups and hosts several blogs. In addition to writing, the author is also an artist, an introverted recluse, a self proclaimed empath and a foodie. Pepper Pace can be contacted at her blog, Writing Feedback:

http://pepperpacefeedback.blogspot.com/ or by email at pepperpace.author@yahoo.com

Baby Girl and the Mean Boss

CPSIA information can be obtained at www.ICGtesting.com
Printed in the USA
LVOW10s1921131214

418709LV00016B/373/P